Coming Up Short
9

CHARLES WELCH

Copyright © 2024 Charles Welch

All rights reserved.

ISBN:

DEDICATION
To all of you who take the time to write **reviews on AMAZON – THANK YOU!!!**

ACKNOWLEDGMENTS

Thank you to my extensive team who make all this work come to life.

FALSE DEPRIVATION

"Hey! You'll never guess what happened!"

Dr. Pam Ettinger listened to her friend and coworker screech her happiness over the phone. She held her Samsung device away from her ear and thumbed the volume down button on the side until she could bear the sound of her friend's voice. Stella Madison wasn't her best, or closest friend, but she was one of a very few people outside of her own family that she could stand to be around for more than a few minutes. They were coworkers together at the Wilthrop Psychological Institution and though they had very different jobs, Pam liked Stella.

Pam earned her doctorate in psychiatry several years ago and specialized in counseling trauma victims. She had come to work for Dr. Wilthrop's clinic for a few reasons, not the least of which was its proximity to her home. A ten-minute drive on any weekday morning would have her in her parking space at the Institute and most often sitting at her desk awaiting the arrival of the day's first patient.

The ability to treat patients dealing with anxiety and PTSD with a variety of treatment options was another reason she joined the clinic. She had everything from psychotherapy and medication to meditation at her disposal, and most of her patients had made significant progress under her care. She even utilized the sensory deprivation pool sometimes if the patient was right for the treatment.

She was still grateful to the old codger, Dr. Wilthrop, for hiring her and she had learned a lot from him, despite his perpetual case of grumpiness. Mark Wilthrop was a stickler for details, although she had seen him bend a few rules occasionally. These instances included situations that, if she had done the same for a patient, he would have scolded her.

Meanwhile, Stella, her coworker, who was their administrative aide, as well as patient financial and insurance advisor, was over the moon excited about a necklace that had arrived out of the blue in her mail.

"And Dr. Ettinger, it's the prettiest piece of jewelry I think I've ever seen. I'm not sure what type of stone it is, but it's a large, smooth black rock at the bottom of a golden chain. It's amazing!"

Pam smiled. She couldn't help it. Though she and Stella weren't super close, she was thrilled the woman thought enough of her to call and share her good fortune. Pam commented, "Black stones are usually, uh let me see If I can remember…" She paused to recall what she knew about precious stones. "If memory serves, and it doesn't so much these days, but anyway, I think black stones can be obsidian, or opal, or onyx, and, umm… wait, I think there are even black pearls. It could really be anything. And you don't know who it's from?"

"No. Isn't that crazy?" Stella squealed again and

Coming Up Short 9

the pitch of her voice rose until Pam was sure only she, and dogs, could hear it. Stella continued, "And here's the weirdest part. It came in a box with a little card that says – Peace comes with forgiveness, but contentment comes with forgetting." Stella seemed to pause to contemplate the written words again. "Isn't that the strangest thing?"

Pam finished rolling out the bread dough she had made from scratch and placed it on a baking sheet with some flour so it wouldn't stick. She'd been making the recipe since her hair was all blonde and absent the gray that recently began to spread on her head like the plague. While she didn't necessarily care about the color of her hair (she wasn't a vain person by nature), she resented the aches that were slowly creeping into her joints. She often thought about only being in her early forties and wondered how she would feel in another decade or two.

Pam replied to Stella while still thinking about the ravages of age. "I've never heard of anyone randomly receiving jewelry they weren't expecting unless they were getting a proposal. That message seems to be positive, so maybe someone wanted to brighten your day with the gift."

Stella scoffed over the phone. It came with a familiar little snort that Pam had grown accustomed to at work. "Since Paul dumped me, I'm afraid no one's keeping me warm at night, so there's no forthcoming proposal here."

"Awe, you'll meet someone. Who knows, maybe you have a secret admirer. That could be where the necklace came from." Pam offered, knowing that Stella wouldn't believe any such thing was possible.

Coming Up Short 9

"No, that's not it. I'm not the kind of girl a guy does that stuff for." Stella typically put herself down.

She was a pretty girl who was slightly overweight, and Pam spent a lot of their casual chats at work trying to build her confidence. Pam worried about Stella and was glad they were getting to know each other better. Pam wanted to ask her who she thought the sender of the piece of jewelry could be, but didn't get the chance.

Stella spoke again, and her words caught her attention. "I know this will sound weird, but…"

"But?"

Stella giggled. "I don't know. It's like when I put this necklace on, I get the strangest vague but pleasant feeling. It's like I feel everything is going to be okay and like I… like I can't remember some things and I don't care that I forgot them."

Pam slid the bread dough into the refrigerator with a towel over it and shut the appliance door. "Are these things you can't remember negative things?"

"Oh, I don't know, I mean I guess so," Stella sighed. "It's so beautiful."

"Wear it tomorrow so I can see it, okay?"

Stella agreed. "I will. I better let you go. Speaking of forgetting things, I need to go to my mom's. She's waiting for me."

"Okay, well, enjoy that necklace, and don't forget too much. I'll see you tomorrow."

★★★

Around a bite of spaghetti and homemade bread, Aaron looked across the table at his wife and asked, "So, Stella claims this necklace has a power of some sort?" He had a curious look on his face, which was impossible for him to pull off without tilting his head at a weird angle. Pam always thought it made him look like a cartoon character. She loved her husband dearly, and part of the reason was that he was so easy to read.

She replied, "That's what she said. I'll have to ask her more about it tomorrow. I was surprised by her call, honestly. I've gotten to know her, but didn't realize she and I were that close."

"It was nice of her, mom," Jenna said. Though only a teenager, Jenna was at the age that she constantly weighed in on her parents' behaviors and choices as though she were the mother, and they were her children. "She obviously likes you more than you like her." Jenna stabbed the air with her fork for emphasis.

"No, that's not true." Pam defended herself. "I like Stella. I just don't know her well."

Jenna, a copy of her mother in many ways, responded with a dose of sarcasm. "And does that have anything to do with you being an important doctor and Stella being a lowly coordinator?"

"Of course not!" Pam scolded her daughter. "You know I'm not like that."

Coming Up Short

"I don't know..." Aaron teased. It was his way of deescalating the tension between his wife and daughter. Pam noticed he did it a lot, which wasn't the best compliment regarding her relationship with Jenna.

She inhaled deeply and changed the subject. "So, since you're both here right now, are we still going to the Santon's next weekend?"

"Yeah, I love it when we hang at the farm." Jenna answered, and she was being honest. In the years they had been close family friends to the Santons, their old neighbors, Jenna loved going to their farm.

"Sounds good to me," Aaron agreed.

"Great." Pam stood from the table and picked up her plate and silverware. "If you'll both excuse me, I'm going to grab a shower before our movie. Is that alright?" she asked, staring into the blue eyes of her teenage daughter.

"You have my permission, ma'am." Jenna played along expertly, knowing her mother was trying to get back into a more friendly tone with her.

"Perfect. I'll be right back." Pam walked to the kitchen and dropped her plate in the sink, knowing Aaron would take care of the dishes while she was in the shower. She left the kitchen and entered the long hall of the bedroom wing of the house. As she approached the master bedroom door, she paused. Jenna's recent tendency to push back at her could be a normal thing, and it could be a sign of trouble. She'd need to keep an eye on her daughter in case there was teenage girl drama going on behind the scenes at school.

Coming Up Short

Pam's focus shifted from thoughts of her daughter to the table that sat at the end of the hall by her bedroom door. It was a dark-stained mahogany piece given to her by her late mother. She'd had it since her mother passed away many years before. She had always loved the table, but wondered why she had stopped to stare at it. Glistening silver handles featured the table's one drawer.

The impulse to grab them and yank the drawer open was overwhelming, but she had no idea why. There was nothing in the drawer she needed or wanted. It was stuffed full of old gloves, a winter cap or two, and not much more. She didn't need to dig through the drawer and had promised her family she'd be back soon for the movie they planned to watch. She knew this, and yet the desire to open the drawer felt all-encompassing. The feeling was odd but present, and the sudden longing made her want to seek the advice of one of the other counselors at the clinic. Normally, she wasn't prone to impulsiveness.

"Don't be ridiculous." Pam pried her eyes away from the table and grabbed her bedroom door handle. She quickly pushed into the room, away from the table, but aware of her strange impulse and already trying to forget about it.

The evening would be fun, and she was looking forward to the time with Aaron and Jenna. Pam forced the weird thoughts about the table away and entered the bathroom, intent on connecting with her daughter after a hot shower.

★★★

Coming Up Short

"I'm telling you, it's true!" Stella diverted her eyes from the computer screen at the clinic's front counter to Pam, who stood next to her. Stella offered a genuine smile. The woman was consumed with the mysterious necklace that had arrived at her house via the mailman, sender unknown.

Stella continued to rattle off positive events she'd experienced since the arrival of the necklace. Her eyes sparkled, and she seemed a lot happier since Pam had last seen her the day before. Stella winked at Pam and added, "I refuse to take it off now because of all the good it's doing me."

"And no clue where it came from?"

"No," Stella answered. "And I don't want to know. All I know is since I put it on, everything I want tends to work out." She grabbed Pam's hand and squeezed it lightly before releasing it. "How do you explain that?"

Pam shrugged. "I guess I can't."

As if she hadn't heard Pam, Stella pressed on, "And I even got a call last night from Paul!"

Pam noted the rising color of good cheer on Stella's pale cheeks. "Who?"

"Paul!" Stella squealed and then hushed herself even though the lobby before them was empty. "Remember my old boyfriend? The one with the dark hair?" She waved a hand at Pam's inability to recall Paul. "He's a jerk. Well, it actually sounds like he's changed. He was so sincere when he called, and he apologized for disappearing on me."

The door chime across the lobby rang and Pam leveled her gaze at the old woman who entered the clinic. She moved in slight but sure steps toward them. Her gray hair bounced atop her head as she gimped along.

"To be continued," Stella muttered as the woman approached.

Stella smiled even broader at the approaching patient and asked, "How are you today, Evelyn?"

"I'm doing fine, young lady. Thank you for asking." Evelyn shifted her black handbag from one arm to the other. Her eyes found Pam, and she addressed her. "Hello, Dr. Ettinger. How are you?"

Pam liked the older woman and had heard from Dr. Wilthrop that she'd made great progress recently and it appeared he was right. The older woman's demeanor was drastically different from the woman who had first come seeking help with her anxiety issues. Pam responded to the older woman, "I'm great. Are you here for a session with Dr. Wilthrop?"

"Yes, I'm getting my anxiety under control and finding ways to relax. It hasn't been easy, but I'm thrilled with how much better I'm doing. You people here are sure doing God's work, I can tell you that. My life has completely changed."

Pam felt genuine emotion in response to Evelyn's words. It felt good to see the work they did have a real impact on their clients. "Well, that is wonderful to hear. One of these days, you might ask Dr. Wilthrop about using the sensory deprivation pool for some deep relaxation. He might approve it for you."

Evelyn wrinkled up her nose and frowned at Pam. "Oh, I could never climb into one of those tanks, no way! Just thinking about being locked in one gets my heart going. I'm claustrophobic. I wouldn't last five seconds."

"It's not one of the small chambers you're talking about. We use a pool here, although the room is dark to deprive sensory stimuli. It really does work to alleviate trauma and anxiety. I have many patients who use it weekly." Pam explained.

Evelyn shook her head and leaned close over the counter. With her voice lowered to a conspiratorial whisper, she said, "I've heard of people who suffer hallucinations and memory loss from being in those contraptions too long." She straightened and said, "It's not for me."

Pam relented, knowing the therapy would never work for someone so against it. "I wouldn't want you to do anything that would make you feel uncomfortable. Like all therapy options, it works for some patients and not others. As for the hallucinations, though, that only happens when a patient is in the deprivation environment for too long."

Stella added, "I know Dr. Wilthrop never allows a patient to go beyond fifteen minutes."

Pam nodded in agreement. "Yes, we limit the time here, although it usually takes a half hour or longer for hallucinations and potential memory loss to occur. Although, it's not so much memory loss as it is memory reprogramming, and that has never been approved by the APA as a form of treatment." She checked the time on her watch and bid both women a good afternoon. "I've got a session soon."

Pam noticed Stella tracking her as she moved around the front desk and across the lobby behind Evelyn. When Pam reached the hall leading to the session rooms, she glanced back over her shoulder to observe Stella for a moment. Stella had always suffered from a lack of confidence, but it would be difficult to discern that now. Pam thought about the sudden return of Stella's ex-boyfriend and made a mental note to ask her about it. It seemed the mystery necklace was affecting all kinds of changes in her friend at work.

★★★

Aaron had been asleep for a while before Pam finally succumbed to the exhaustion of her day. She drifted into sleep with the TV showing reruns of an old sitcom. It hung on the bedroom wall opposite their bed. It was often the device she used to distract her busy mind until sleep rescued her from the rigors of her day, though she knew better than to use TV as a sleep aid. It wasn't the best way to get a restful sleep, but what her patients and Dr. Wilthrop didn't know wouldn't hurt her.

As Pam's breathing slowed, she drifted into a scene in which she stood in her front yard. A feeling of relief came over her. Whatever had come before was behind her now, and it was time to shut down her worries. That thing, that stressful event, or person, or whatever had caused her to feel such awful tension, was now far away in another universe, and that was indeed good news.

Thoughts of her fears and anxieties drifted away into the blue afternoon sky. Soon, she was only a woman enjoying a brilliantly sunny day in her front yard. Gone were the worries over her and Aaron's relationship losing its romantic spark and the dread she felt over Jenna growing further and further away from her. Long gone was that other dark, devious, and evil memory that poked at the edge of her conscious mind. It was something of substance, and something awful, but in this bright, happy place, it was only a vague notion. She couldn't recall it, and for that she was grateful.

For now, she stood as warm rays of sunshine fell to darken her skin. A person could only stress about something for so long before they needed a mental break, and this place, this sleep-altered version of her yard, provided that condition. On this beautiful sunny day, there was no bad news and nothing that could arise out of the blue to destroy her universe.

Pam smiled and waved at her neighbor, Jan, who was walking down her driveway to the mailbox. The heavy-set woman with short jet-black hair moved along as though she had all the time in the world to retrieve whatever gifts the universe had blessed her with that day. Though Aaron wasn't the biggest fan of Jan, Pam had always been nice to her. He disliked her dry, nosey personality and thus commented on everything about the woman. He even poked fun at Jan's obvious hair color enhancement.

While it was true she colored her hair, and Pam agreed with him that the dark shade didn't help to hide

Coming Up Short 9

her advanced years, she still told him to be nice. Jan wasn't the only woman in the world not in love with the aging process.

Pam watched the older woman slow-walk her way down her drive. She was heading to the mailbox but didn't seem to be in a rush. Pam knew she had already recognized the slow movements of her neighbor, but she couldn't understand why. Didn't everyone hurry to their mailbox?

This thought sparked a desire in Pam to check her mail, and she moved across her low-cut lawn. Under her bare feet, individual blades of green tickled her soles and the underside of her toes. It felt good to have the mental capacity to notice something so small and irrelevant, and to find joy in the sensation. How much of life had she missed due to being consumed with the material and stressful parts of life? She wondered how many little miracles of the world had come and gone without her notice.

The world could be a demanding place, but it could also be beautiful. As long as the horrible thing she couldn't recall stayed away, it would be a wonderful day in the sun.

Pam shifted her focus back to her mailbox.

The mailman, Rusty was his name if she remembered correctly, typically came in the morning so there should be something in the small, skinny black box. For the moment, there seemed to be no more worthy task in the universe than finding out who thought enough of her to reach out with a handwritten letter, or a flyer for the local market's sale items, or even a political ad attempting to sway her vote. The more she thought about it, the more she appreciated the concept of the mail.

It was a tradition that she hoped technology wouldn't someday completely eradicate. All the email and instant messages in the world would never replace the act of sending someone physical mail. The joy in pulling paper and packages from the mailbox, with nothing in her heart but curiosity, was something special, and yet it was another component of life she had never taken the time to adequately appreciate.

Pam wondered why it had taken her so long to contemplate the job Rusty did six days a week and it was her intention to express her thanks to him the next time she saw him out and about in his blue uniform and little red, white, and blue jeep. He had an important job. Who knew how many people relied on him every day to deliver to them the things they needed; the things they craved? As far as she was concerned, it was incalculable.

While she moved down the lawn, Pam kept her eyes on Jan, who had still not returned her friendly gesture. The older woman moved toward her mailbox, toward the road that separated their yards, with stoic resignation spread across her pretty face.

Pam arrived at her mailbox first and waited until Jan also reached the edge of the road. Again, Pam raised a hand and waved at her neighbor. In addition to the gesture, she yelled. "Nice day!"

Jan arrived at her mailbox (as black and narrow as Pam's) and, with one last footstep, came to a halt. She raised her eyes and stared across the road at Pam without a hint of the friendliness Pam had extended. Not only was the woman's face a blank slate, but there was also no recognition in her eyes. It was as though Pam were a friendly, yet overzealous stranger.

A small part of Pam wanted to be offended. Another, larger part knew better.

As her mother had taught her at an early age, if she at first did not succeed in gaining the attention of her neighbor, she would try, try again. "Hello, Jan! Isn't it a lovely day?" Again, she offered the cheerful wave of her right hand.

In response, Jan only stood, vacant, staring back at her. The woman was a completely unoccupied vessel. She was a person so bored with her life that she might not fully be aware she still lived.

Knowing it would do no good to wave again, Pam gave up and turned to her mailbox. Jan had become as still, and immovable, as a statue. Maybe she had just come home from a medical procedure and was still not completely removed from the effects of anesthesia.

"Oh, well." Pam pulled the small, hinged door to her mailbox open, and at first, felt her heart sink. Her eyes told her there was nothing inside, that no one had thought enough of her to reach out even with a bill that was past due.

She was ready to feel sorry for herself, but the idea she should change her angle and peek deeper into the darkness came upon her. Sometimes, Rusty got in a hurry and shoved her mail further back than was necessary. She bent her knees, forgetting for a moment about Jan, and peered into the darkness of the slender mail slot.

Her eyes found a small square tan box sitting in the darkness as though it was a planet floating in the nothingness of a small universe. She reached into the seemingly endless pit and withdrew a cube that fit neatly in the palm of her hand.

In the daylight, the small box seemed far less evil than it had at the back of the mailbox. Pam noted its smooth cover and the crisp seams at each of its corners. "It's so nice!" She was delighted that someone had thought enough of her to drop a gift in her mailbox and wondered if it had been Aaron who was responsible for the cute little surprise.

The package had no label on it and no return address. It was as anonymous a gift as she had ever received. "Wow! This is so unexpected. I'm thrilled!"

Remembering that Jan was still on the other side of the road, Pam turned in a half circle. Across the street, her neighbor woman stood in the exact same place as she had been all along. The door to her mailbox was still closed, however, Jan held her right hand out toward Pam. On her palm sat an identical tan box.

This revelation puzzled her. "You got one too?"

Though Jan didn't respond to her, other than to continue staring, Pam eliminated Aaron as the giver of her small gift. If it had been him, he wouldn't have also given one to Jan. He didn't even like the older neighbor woman. He thought she was a nosey old biddy.

Coming Up Short 9

Pam's eyes fell away from Jan, and she stared at a crack in the middle of her tan box. Had it been there before?

She was unsure, but had probably overlooked it in her glee. This was where it would open. Most likely, the little line was where the top would separate from the base, pivoting on a pair of tiny hinges hidden under the tan fabric.

Clutching the top of the box in one hand and the base in the other, Pam pulled. As anticipated, it opened at its mid-point until the lid lifted as far as it would go. "Oh, my God! It's gorgeous!" She stared down at a necklace composed of a gold chain and a black stone. The stone was as deep and dark as a summer night sky and sparkled as much as the stars shined down.

A thought entered her mind. She had seen the piece of expensive jewelry before somewhere, but the thought flitted away before she could truly explore it.

After removing the necklace from the box, and holding it up to shine in the sun, Pam once again diverted her attention to Jan.

Her neighbor woman stood staring at her still, but now, she also held her necklace out. Pam was right. It was an identical piece to the one clutched in her hand. Jan continued to stare as if not seeing her. The woman's face remained a blank slate. She had received a gift in the mail, and though she held it up to display it to Pam, she seemed not to have a care in the world. Not even an ounce of curiosity about its origins crossed Jan's mind.

"They're beautiful, aren't they?" Pam asked her

neighbor. "We're so lucky." She unclasped the chain and slipped it around her neck before reconnecting the chain. The little black stone rested against the exposed skin on the V of her buttoned top. It felt cool against her chest. A wave of peace overcame her. "That's so nice. Everything will be alright now." She heard herself and was pleased at how relaxed she sounded. Things were going to work out. Her stresses and worries would soon be gone. She could tell. Even the secret hidden thing would now be forever forgotten. She felt the piece of jewelry warm her from head to toe. "It's as amazing as it is beautiful."

Like the horn from an oncoming freight train, Jan opened her mouth and screamed at Pam. "What does it mean?" The old woman's eyes had taken on the blazing hatred of an angered viper. She sneered at Pam. Spittle flew from her mouth as she held the necklace out with a shaking hand. "What does this mean? Why do you have it, Pam?"

"I...I...don't..."

"Why?" Jan pleaded with her through an impossibly loud voice. Though her elderly neighbor didn't strain to scream, her voice was loud enough that it hurt to hear.

"Please stop!" Pam staggered back, away from the road. The sunny day she had stepped into had evaporated. The sky was now overcast and threatening. "You're hurting me." Pam's hand found the pendant at her neck and held it. Happy vibrations worked into her arm. "Please..."

"Why, Pam? Why do you have that?" Jan's

voice was drifting away as though she were speeding off in a fast-moving car.

Pam's eyes searched for her neighbor again, only to see she had gone. "What happened? Where'd she go…"

Pam sat up in her bed, clutching at her neck. Awareness settled over her. She wore no necklace and everything that occurred with her neighbor had only been a dream. She sighed. While her dream version of Jan had been stressful, she missed the feel of the necklace around her neck. The sensation of peace it brought had been nothing short of amazing and wonderful. "It's Stella's not mine."

She ran a hand through her hair and swiveled from under the covers. Behind her, Aaron dozed peacefully. She reviewed the nightmare. "It's the stress coming through. Your subconscious mind is trying to settle something." As a psychologist, she knew this was true. As a person, it bothered her she couldn't figure out what had triggered the stressful sleep event.

"And the necklace I clearly adopted into the dream because of Stella." This much was obvious. She picked up the glass of water on her night table and swallowed vigorously. There was still time for rest if she could get her mind off the wicked dream.

★★★

"I don't know, Dr. Ettinger. Sometimes I feel so lost without her, and when I do, it helps me to…" Natalie Cross dropped her gaze to her hands in her lap. She intertwined her fingers and released them.

Coming Up Short 9

"Talk to her?" Pam asked.

"Yes. Does that make me crazy?" The young woman with the beautiful mane of dark hair returned her eyes to Pam. "I loved Sheila like a sister."

"No, it means you're trying to cope with the loss of your friend."

"Should I try to stop doing it?" Natalie questioned. "I mean, at some point, I have to move on, right?"

Pam truly felt empathetic toward her patient. "You'll know when it's time to move on. Don't force yourself into anything."

"It's just that my husband has caught me talking to an empty room a few times, and it worries him," Natalie explained.

"Tell him what I said. It's a coping mechanism and you need to roll with it for a while. This loss of yours, and the pain it's caused, is still fresh. These things take time. The two of you had been friends for quite a while." Pam leaned forward. "Don't allow anyone to pressure you into things that make you feel uncomfortable, even your husband."

Natalie nodded. "Yeah, okay. I like it when I chat with her. Sometimes it's like she's really there with me, you know?"

"I understand." Pam thought for a moment about the idea of using the sensory deprivation pool as a part of Natalie's treatment.

Coming Up Short 9

"I guess as long as I remember she isn't really there, it's okay."

"Natalie, how would you feel about using our sensory deprivation pool as a part of your therapy?"

Natalie glanced at her again. "What would that do?"

"It's a pool of body temperature water we use. It's saline water. You get in the pool, which is only three feet deep, and float on the surface. We put earplugs in and blackout goggles over your eyes, so we eliminate all sensory input. The room is sound-deadened and has minimal light. The idea is to allow your brain to isolate on its issues and focus on them. It accelerates emotional healing from trauma. The treatment has been very successful, and it would help you come to terms with your loss. Eventually, with a few treatments, you'd be able to say goodbye to your friend." Pam smiled at her. "You'd only be in the pool for ten minutes, although it will seem to be much longer. How does that sound?"

Natalie stiffened in her chair. She stared intently at Pam. Her voice became defensive as she spoke. "While I want to watch how much I talk to her, I don't want to stop entirely. I miss her. I need her here with me still."

"I know what that feels like." Pam muttered.

"Do you? Have you ever lost someone so close?"

Pam winced and stood. Sheila had hit a sore spot (though she didn't know why) and she wanted nothing more than to be alone for a few minutes. "Well, that's all the time we have for today. I'll see you next week." She moved to her office door and opened it. "Think about the pool, and if you change your mind, let me know."

★★★

"How was your session?" Stella appeared at Pam's open office door after Natalie departed.

"Good, she's coming along." Pam waved Stella into her office. "I keep meaning to ask you to show me your surprise necklace."

Stella smiled brightly at the mention of the piece of jewelry and skipped to Pam's desk. She reached into the neckline of her top and pulled at a gold chain with a black oval stone at the bottom. The stone was set into a gold base. Pam touched a fingertip to the stone and shivered as a chill crawled up her hand into her arm. "It's wonderful."

A fractured piece of her dream returned. Pam recalled holding the necklace up to kiss the sun. How it had sparkled in her hand. It had brought her such peace and beauty and…

"Yes, it makes me feel good and I've been sleeping like a baby since I got it," Stella said. Her voice quieted until it dropped to a whisper.

Pam withdrew her touch from the dark rock and watched as Stella tucked it away under her top. A remote part of her was envious that Stella alone got to feel the wonders of the necklace. It seemed almost selfish.

Coming Up Short 9

With it gone from sight, Pam felt a return to herself. The strange emotions of the past minute were alien to her, and she resented them. It wasn't in her character to act envious for no reason. Obviously, Stella had developed an emotional attachment to the necklace and was giving the small black obsidian, or whatever it was, far too much credit for being something other than a polished stone.

While returning to her desk chair, she asked Stella, "Is everything going alright? Aside from the necklace, I mean."

"Yes! And Paul might be coming over in the next couple of days! Everything is going so well now. I'm thrilled."

At the mention of Paul, Pam flashed on something dark, ugly, and deeply sad. Before she could understand the feeling, it was gone. "That's good to hear."

"Are you okay, Dr. Ettinger? You got very pale." Stella watched her as she sat back in her chair.

The concern in Stella's eyes was genuine, and Pam appreciated her for it, although she would never be able to explain the emotions that had sailed through her head. "Yes, yes, fine."

"Good, you scared me for a moment." Stella offered her a sympathetic smile. "You reminded me of my…my…"

Pam watched as the smile on Stella's face faded away and was replaced by a vacancy. Something had been on the tip of her tongue but had abandoned her. Now, the woman stood chasing a fleeting thought.

"Maybe it should be me asking if you're alright." Pam teased.

The emptiness in Stella's eyes slipped away. She forced a grin and said, "Oh, I had a thought, but I spaced it. I do that more and more often. Aging is a terrible thing."

Pam understood, and replied, "Yeah, I've heard that exact expression from my husband…uh…" Pam sighed. "Geez, apparently forgetting things is catching. I can't believe I spaced his name…" She snapped her fingers. "Aaron, his name is Aaron. God, what's wrong with us today?"

Stella laughed. The color returned to her face. "At least it's not only me."

"Right. So, how did your mom react to Paul returning to your life?" Pam inquired as a means of changing the subject, but also out of curiosity.

"My mom?"

"Yes, weren't you going to tell your mother about Paul calling you?" Pam didn't like the strange expression of distance that had come over Stella. Again, her eyes dulled, and her face seemed as though she had lost all ability to smile or frown. Pam asked, "What's wrong?"

Stella seemed to shake herself free of the malaise that had overcome her. "I don't have a mom. I've never had a mother."

Before Pam could question their previous conversation, Stella turned away and exited the office.

★★★

"I swear she referenced her mother the last time I spoke with her." Pam set her fork on her plate and stared across the table at her husband. "Isn't that weird?"

Aaron swallowed a bite of his steak and sipped some water. Pam had always thought he was a theatric eater but never picked at him about it. She had learned to wait for him. It elongated their conversations, but if she complained, he'd tell her she was too demanding and needed to learn to relax. Aaron set his glass on the table and finally replied, "Maybe you should put on your Dr. Ettinger hat and think about it that way instead of your friend at work hat." He nodded once, satisfied with his advice, and returned to eating.

"Fair." Pam considered what he said. "That's actually a good point."

Jenna spoke to her father, "Dad, now you're supposed to say – Yes, I know because I said it!"

Aaron laughed. "If I pulled that with your mother, I get punched later when you're not here to save me."

Pam watched the two of them go back and forth with each other. They were her heart. The love she felt for them both made all life's challenges worthwhile. Without them, she would be nothing. She hated herself for the tears that forced their way into her eyes, but there was no denying them. They had arrived to make her look like an overly emotional woman.

"Geez, mom." Jenna giggled. "What's wrong with you?"

"Nothing…" Pam wiped at her eyes.

"Are you alright, honey?" Aaron asked from the other end of the table.

Pam felt she owed them an explanation for her sudden moment of emotional reflection. "I'm fine. I guess I just love you both so much. The sentiment carried me away for a second there."

"We love you too, honey," Aaron affirmed.

Pam couldn't shake the desire she felt to protect them. "I wouldn't know what to do without you two."

"Well, I'll be around, being a pain in the ass for a few more years Mom, so don't worry," Jenna said in her off-hand teenage way.

"I hope you stay as long as we can keep you here," Pam said, and used her napkin to pat her eyes. The idea she would forever be lost without them wouldn't leave her mind. "Please be careful, okay?"

Aaron asked her, "Are you worried about something specific?"

It occurred to her she was supposed to be the

mental health professional. Aaron was guiding her through her emotions better than she did most of her patients, which was embarrassing. Her husband was no psychologist. For a living he worked in... Pam stared across the table at him. She prodded at her mind regarding his profession. "What the hell is wrong with me?"

Jenna waved her fork at her before taking another bite. "You're probably premenopausal. It happens to the best of us in time."

"You look like you're trying to remember something," Aaron observed.

"No." Pam would never admit to him that she couldn't recall what he did for a living. She didn't want him to worry about her. "I'm good. Just be careful."

★★★

Pam spent the next morning updating patient files with her notes from the previous day's sessions. At ten o'clock, Stella popped into her office. "Hi, Dr. Ettinger, do you have a minute?"

"Sure." Pam typed the last line of notes into a file and saved the document. "Come on in."

"Thank you." Stella approached the desk and sat in a chair opposite her.

Pam pulled the reading glasses from her nose and set them on her desk. "How are you, Stella?"

Coming Up Short 9

"I'm fine, but I wanted to share some exciting news with you!" Stella clapped her hands in anticipation.

"What is it?"

Stella leaned close to the desk as though she had a secret to share, although Pam was certain her coworker had already shared it with most of the staff. Stella squealed as she said, "Paul and I are going to restart our relationship! I'm so happy!"

Pam smiled and congratulated Stella. "So, you mentioned you are restarting your relationship, as in, you were previously in a relationship with Paul?"

"That's right, although my mom never liked him. I'll have to break the news to her later."

Pam liked Stella, and she felt sorry for her. It was hard when a parent didn't support one's life choices. She asked Stella, "How will you tell her?" She tried recalling if she had heard Stella complain about her mother before and came up blank.

With a sigh, Stella said, "I'll just come out with it." She stood from Pam's office chair. "I better get back to the front desk. It was important for me to share my news with you. You've always been so kind to me."

"Thank you so much for sharing, you're a sweetheart." As Stella left her office, Pam reopened a window on her desktop computer. She couldn't escape the feeling she was forgetting something of importance about her kind coworker.

After performing an employee file search for

Coming Up Short 9

Stella Madison, she opened the document that came up and began reading. In a short amount of time, Pam concluded Stella had been a superior employee with no documented cases of being late to work or failing to perform the duties of her job. From everything she could see, Stella was as kind as she seemed. Dr. Wilthrop had performed all her evaluations and had even promoted her a couple of times already.

"Hmm. I must be losing it." With a sigh, Pam closed the file and turned off the computer. It had already been a long day, and it was only half over.

★★★

"You look tired. You should try working less so you can get some rest." Aaron massaged her shoulders for a minute before he walked away. "I'm going to bed. You should call it a night and come too."

"I know, you're right." Pam glanced at the clock in their living room from where she sat on the sofa. It was already a quarter to midnight. She shut off her laptop and followed Aaron down the hall to their bedroom. On her way through the door, she hesitated by the antique table at the end of the hall.

It called out to her, and she hesitated. There was something about it she found troubling. She had never wanted to do anything more than she wanted to open the small drawer in the table, and yet, she found the idea terrifying. "Leave me alone," Pam whispered as she moved into her room and shut her bedroom door on the old piece of furniture.

★★★

Coming Up Short 9

"Hey, Pam. Do you have a minute?"

Pam shifted her gaze from the document she was signing to Dr. Wilthrop, who stood in her open office door. The older man was smiling at her, but that meant nothing. She had once told him if he hadn't gone into a career in mental health, he could have been one hell of a poker player. Though she would never admit it to him, she loved his professional demeanor and even envied it. He seemed unshakeable and confident to the point she didn't believe he'd ever had a single moment of self-doubt in his life.

"Sure." She watched him cross the room to her. He was mostly bald, and what hair he had was white. It matched the snowy hair on his chin and only lent credibility to the orderly man he was.

Wilthrop sat in one of the cozy chairs on the other side of the desk and crossed his legs. For a man of his age, he was in remarkable shape. He asked, "How are things going?"

Pam laughed. "In a general sense or are we having an unplanned session?" Her laughter was slightly defensive, and he knew it. It was in the way he looked at her with a combination of concern and sympathy.

He folded his hands together over one knee, and without changing his expression said, "You avoided the question. Was that on purpose?"

Pam felt her face flush. "No, not at all. I'm fine. Why do you ask?"

His face crumpled into a slight frown and then was gone as fast as it had come. "You seem a little off lately, distracted perhaps."

Pam faced him directly. She knew it was important to be direct with the doctor. "No, just busy. Did I miss getting you something you needed?"

He waved her off and refolded his hands. "No, no nothing like that. Maybe a better way to say this is, you seem tired, maybe a bit worn down. Is your caseload too much right now? I know you've taken on most of our new patients recently and I apologize for that. I'm engaged in some research that has siphoned quite a lot of my time."

"Honestly, I'm doing fine. I have been tired lately, but nothing I can't handle." Pam glanced at her open office door and lowered her voice. "Can you tell me about the research you're involved with?"

"I'm afraid not. I signed an NDA." His expression still did not change.

"I see." Pam smiled despite Wilthrop shutting her out of his research. "Well, to answer your question, I'm fine and my caseload is totally manageable."

Dr. Wilthrop stood. "It might do you some good to make use of the sens dep pool. Of course, you already know that."

"I might." The idea of a few minutes of relaxation was more than appealing to her.

Coming Up Short 9

"Make sure you have someone to watch the timer. Nothing longer than ten to fifteen minutes."

While Pam resented that he felt he needed to remind her of the pool protocols, she kept her mouth shut. "Of course." She watched him step away from her desk. He was almost at her office door when she asked. "Dr. Wilthrop?"

He turned to her. "Yes?"

"Is everything alright with Stella Madison?"

He shrugged. "I spoke with her earlier and she seemed fine. Is there something I should know about?"

"No, I had a funny feeling about her earlier, but I'm sure it meant nothing." She offered a smile to reassure him and keep him from pressing further about Stella.

"We should listen to our instincts. If anything else comes up, let me know. I've known her for a long time. I can nose around without seeming too obvious." The smile he offered was more than she had ever seen him give anyone. While she wanted to believe he was genuine, she felt as if she now knew what it would be like to get a friendly grin from a rattlesnake.

★★★

After her last patient session of the day, Pam got an idea and intended to follow through on it before her weary mind moved on to other things and she forgot.

Coming Up Short 9

She intentionally waited until she worked an hour past the office closing time and then sauntered to the lobby to see if Stella was still around or if one of the custodians was in sight.

The lobby appeared empty which was exactly as she wanted it to be.

"Dr. Ettinger? Why in the world are you still here?" The voice came from behind her.

Pam spun on her heel to come face to face with Stella. "Oh, Stella! You startled me!"

"I'm sorry." Stella offered. "I was on my way out. Did you need anything?"

"Oh, no. I'm going to leave soon too. I need to do one more thing in my office and then I'm out of here." She moved past her coworker. If Stella followed her, the plans she had designed would go up in smoke. "Have a good evening." The smile she offered was less than honest but got the job done. Stella said goodnight and crossed the lobby to the exit.

After waiting in the hall, out of sight, Pam confirmed Stella's leaving and then scurried to the storage room where paper files existed on all past patients. Dr. Wilthrop insisted on records that were not electronic once a patient was no longer active with the institution.

She used her key and slipped into the room that wasn't far up the hall from her office. Overhead fluorescent lights blinked to life, and she stared at a wall of stored file boxes. Each of the boxes was gray and had a red label on it indicating the first letter of former patients last names.

All the boxes were stacked in front of her. The A boxes were on her far left. The Z boxes ended the row and were located at the far-right end of the room.

"There's more of them than I imagined." She stared up at the top row of the boxes. The entire wall looked like a downtown brick building.

Moving to the boxes indicating last names beginning with M, in the center of the wall, she chastised herself for her nosiness. The hunch she was playing was a long shot. Hopefully, she would quickly see how wrong she was, and she'd be able to move on, understanding there was no conspiracy afoot at her place of employment.

"Okay, Stella Madison, let's make sure you don't have a patient file here." The thought, expressed out loud, made her feel more stupid than she felt before hearing it.

"Stupider." It was a real word although she hadn't believed it when…

Pam stopped and squeezed her eyes shut against the room. She seethed at herself. "He's your fucking husband for God's sake!" Her mind pressed forward, searching desperately for the inner file that would remind her of the man she married. It finally arrived in a flash. "Aaron! Dammit!"

Coming Up Short 9

Pam opened her eyes, relief flooding her veins. Aaron was her husband, and Jenna was her daughter. Aaron was the person who had told her stupider was a real word. The same Aaron who was her husband and the same guy she couldn't remember. "God, I'm ridiculous." It wasn't like she'd been married five times and had five children with each husband. There were only two of them. "It's ridiculous."

She focused on the task at hand. Her feet carried her to four boxes, all of which had been labeled with a large M on their sides. "Alright, let's get this done." She grabbed the top box, assuming if Stella Madison was in the files as a former patient, she would appear in the first box. The second letter of her last name was A, so it was a good theory.

After taking the box down from the pile, and setting it at her feet, she popped the lid off and stared into the labeled file tabs that protruded at the top of the box.

The first patient in the box was a woman – MacDonald, Lisa.

Pam flicked to the next file. "I'll be damned." Her stomach sank as she reread the handwritten name on the file.

She plucked the file labeled, Madison, Stella, free of the box and plopped it on the floor. She'd apologize to her husband for being late via a text message shortly. First, she had a file to read.

Coming Up Short 9

***

Pam sat on the floor of the storage closet in disbelief over the things she'd read in Stella's patient file. Her mind whirled through so many different bits of information and feelings. She snapped the cover closed on the file and shoved it back into its slot in the box. There was no reason to read through all the secrets it contained for a fourth time.

What she desired to do, deep in her heart, was to confront Wilthrop with everything she'd learned, but she'd never do it. If he perceived she was challenging him on his decisions, she'd find herself looking for another job somewhere else. While too many things had happened for her to look past, there were other ways of addressing the situation.

She also had some curiosities regarding Stella and Dr. Wilthrop.

First, it was odd that Wilthrop had never mentioned Stella was a patient in the past. Neither had Stella. Provider and patient confidentiality were a reality, but Wilthrop wouldn't have violated any laws by telling her Stella received treatment in the clinic. The man clearly wanted to keep that information to himself.

She felt sure she knew why too. Stella seemed to be leading a life of delusion which meant that Wilthrop had failed his patient. The boyfriend Stella kept going on about, Paul, from her past, dumped Stella several years before. That much was true. According to Wilthrop's notes, Paul had disappeared from Stella's life at a pivotal moment.

Pam climbed to her feet. She considered her recent conversation with Stella and understood the seriousness of Stella's current mental health. The poor woman was in bad shape.

After clicking off the light and exiting the small room, Pam texted Aaron saying she was on her way home. She returned to her office to grab her things and further contemplate Stella. Something had gone seriously wrong with the treatment Wilthrop had given Stella. He'd used a combination of drug and sensory deprivation pool therapy and had concluded in his notes that Stella was now engaged with reality. He'd gone so far as to say she'd reached a stage of normalcy and self-actualization.

"Yeah, right." After gathering her car keys, Pam clicked off her office light and entered the hallway. She would need to decide how to handle the most alarming component of Stella's file. "Her mother died. She killed herself before Paul left."

Stella's mother was gone, and yet, Stella indicated she would soon tell her mother about her recent reconnection with Paul. Pam would need to confront her coworker with this information and gauge her reaction.

Stella wasn't well, and there was something going on with Wilthrop. "Stella needs help."

Another thought popped into her mind as she

walked. "Paul probably isn't back in the picture either. Dear God, Stella may be completely delusional and in need of substantial cognitive behavioral therapy."

***

Aaron wanted to sleep. She knew this but couldn't stop rambling on about her concerns over Stella and Dr. Wilthrop. He had the covers pulled up to his chin and was lying on his side, which was the position he assumed to fall asleep every night.

He was a good man and hadn't yet complained about the bedside lamp that she still had turned on. She appreciated him listening to her carrying on about the issues at work. She needed to verbalize the issue to sort it through.

"I'm serious, Aaron, she's delusional and I didn't pick up on it." She turned to face him. "What kind of shrink am I?"

"You weren't treating her. Why would you notice?" He blinked his eyes against his coming sleep. "Anyway, you did figure it out if you think about it. We're having this discussion because you followed a hunch and checked the past patient files, right?"

She paused, "Yeah, I hadn't considered that, but it's a good point." She smiled for a second. "Thank you for that."

"Sure, babe."

"I also think I've figured something else out. I think Stella found a necklace, the one she keeps talking about, and she's using it as this mystical, powerful harbinger of extraordinary things to come because her mind can't handle that her mother and her old boyfriend are gone." She sighed. "And that means Wilthrop completely fucked up her treatment."

Aaron yawned and squeezed his eyes shut against the light of her lamp. "What are you going to do about it?"

"I'm sorry, I know I'm keeping you up." Pam slid out of the bed and grabbed her robe from the chair beside their bed. "I'll figure it out."

"Where are you going?" he asked through another yawn.

She leaned over the bed and kissed his cheek, feeling his whiskers poke her tender lips. "I can't sleep so I'm going to go do some thinking and let you rest up."

Pam clicked off the lamp and crossed the room, pausing as she opened their door to glance back at him. "And…" Aaron was already asleep. "Never mind sleeping beauty."

Intending to make some tea and relax in the living room, Pam pulled her bedroom door closed and stepped into the hall. She pivoted away from her bedroom and froze in place in the hall. Her eyes stared down at the antique table from her mother at the end of the hall.

Coming Up Short 9

Before becoming fully aware of what she was doing, Pam reached for the drawer handle on the front of the table. Her fingertips touched the cool metal and then withdrew as if she'd been bitten by a rabid dog. "Why can't you leave me alone?" She hissed at the piece of furniture.

The table did not answer her, but its desire was there. It wanted her to pull its drawer open, and yet, she couldn't get herself to do it. Something bad and rotten lay in the drawer waiting for her. It was biding its time and would do so forever if that's what was required. Eventually, it would get her to do its bidding, and she knew she would fail to resist it when the moment was most crucial.

Pam hurried away from the table, down the hall, and to her kitchen. She forced the feeling of impending doom from her mind. As she made her tea, she considered the sensory deprivation pool at the clinic. There were many positive attributes of the treatment, and she had even utilized it with patients who raved about the clarity and help it gave them. "Maybe it's what I need."

★★★

"Hi, Stella. How are things going with Paul?" The question was the easiest way into the conversation Pam wanted to have with her troubled coworker. Stella sat at the computer terminal at the front desk in the clinic lobby.

Coming Up Short 9

Stella smiled as Pam approached the desk, and answered, "He's so sweet. He's not like before. All the anger he had in him is gone now."

To Pam, it felt as if the warm blue lobby walls were shrinking. They were closing in and would do so until they came together crushing the air from her chest and the spirit from her body. She hated to bring up what she'd read in the work file, but delusional people needed to be forced to see the truth, or they'd spend a lifetime living one lie after another. Pam set her stress aside. Knowing she was about to take the lid off a giant can of worms wouldn't deter her. It was best for Stella to live in reality, rather than the lie she had created about her life. To initiate the discussion, Pam asked her, "How did your mom take the news?"

Pam disliked the glance she received from Stella. In it, was a distance as far away as the moon and stars. The woman had flinched at the mention of her mother. It was a sign that her subconscious mind knew the truth.

Stella's eyes found Pam's, "You know I don't have a mother, right?"

"Is that what you truly believe?" Pam asked.

"Why wouldn't I? It's the truth. I never had one." Stella questioned.

Pam stepped back from the desk. "I want to show you something. Come with me." When Stella didn't move and only stared back with a subtle curiosity, Pam added, "Come on. You need to see this, Stella."

Coming Up Short 9

Stella stood and followed her down the long hallway to the storage room where the files of past patients were stored. She moved along behind Pam as though she were being led to the gallows.

While Pam unlocked the door, Stella spoke with a quiver in her voice. "I don't think we should go in there. Dr. Wilthrop won't like it. He always says to stay out of this room."

"Today, Dr. Wilthrop can shove what he wants up his…well, you know…" Pam trailed off as she opened the door and flicked on the lights. Immediately, she saw the box with the letter M on its side that she sought. Pam held the door open for Stella and ushered her inside. "This will stay between us two, okay?"

Stella trepidatiously stepped into the room, cringing as she did. "Why are we here?"

Pam closed the door after them and moved to the stack of boxes. She pulled the box she was after from the top of the stack and placed it on the floor. After removing the lid from the box, she plucked Stella's file free and opened it. "I wanted to show you this."

After finding the part she wanted Stella to read, Pam flipped the file around and presented it to the dark-headed woman. "You know this room is only for the storage of paper copies of past patient files."

"Yeah." Stella appeared to be on the verge of puking. Her nerves were frayed, and she lacked the capacity to hide her fears. Pam saw it all written across her face as though someone had scrawled on her cheeks and forehead with a big marker.

Pam knew the best approach with someone in deep denial over tragedy was to address the circumstance head-on. She tapped the tab on the file. "What does that say?"

Stella's face crumpled into a frown. "What's the meaning of this? I work here! I'm not a patient!"

Though she was upset, Stella needed to hear what Pam had to say. Pam would make sure she confronted the delusion Stella created. Pam answered, "You work here now, but apparently that wasn't always the case. You were here before as a patient, and this is your patient file." She tapped the interior of the file as she spoke. "You need to read it."

Stella scanned the page for a minute, her face screwing itself into a tight scowl.

"It says you had a mother. You two were very close and it was devastating to you when she…"

"Stop it!" Stella recoiled from her. "You just stop it right now!"

Pam pressed ahead as she'd been trained to do. "Stella, she killed herself." Pam placed an arm on Stella's shoulder to offer comfort. "I'm sorry to tell you that."

"This can't be," Stella mumbled.

"But it is. You had a mother, Stella. Paul left you

shortly after your mom died." Through the fabric of her blouse, nervous ticks in Stella's muscles vibrated Pam's hand. Pam asked her, "Stella, is Paul really back? Have you spoken to him?"

"Yes!" Stella shrugged off her hand. "I've been talking to him!" She pointed at Pam. "And furthermore, you know I grew up without a mother! This…this…file of yours is all nonsense!" Tears welled in her eyes, and she pivoted away from Pam.

"Stella, relax and come back, please," Pam called after her as Stella flung the storeroom door open.

Stella glanced over her shoulder as she departed the storage area. Her face had filled red with anger. With her eyes narrowed to little seams, she spoke. "I don't want to hear about this again." Her words were frosty cold and intended to warn Pam away from the subject.

★★★

While waiting for Aaron and Jenna to return, Pam cleaned the few dishes she found in the kitchen sink and wiped down the counters. Her husband and daughter should be home soon, and when they arrived, she would tell them of her desire to go out for dinner. It had been a rough, emotional day of therapy with her patients, and the interaction she'd had with Stella was the frosting on her stress cake. It had drained her.

After drying her hands, she moved out of the kitchen and stood on the threshold of the living room. On her left, was the long hall to her bedroom. There, deep in the shadows, was the antique table from her mother. She didn't need to see every angle of the piece to know it was there with its simple, yet elegant design features.

"And the drawer," she muttered, feeling very much like she was but a plaything of the table. It had been calling her for days (years?) and it was becoming harder and harder to resist. Pam faced the hall and stared into the darkness. Something dark lived deep inside the drawer in the table.

She stepped forward ignoring the shudder that crawled up her spine. "I'm tired of fighting you…" The words came from her mouth, and she heard them but didn't understand where they came from. She had knowledge buried deep inside that she repressed. It was buried intentionally because… "Because it's awful."

With what seemed to be no more than a blink of her eyes, she stood before the table. She had no memory of walking down the hall. She had been in the living room and then she was here, at this place of terror, her hand already on the drawer handle. She didn't want to open it. No, she would never want to reveal the evil within, but this time, it wasn't up to her.

Already, the drawer was halfway open. Gloves and winter hats lay folded inside as she expected.

"It's under them." She muttered while gazing down at the fully open drawer and its contents. The source of deep stress and worry lay there, just under a pair of black leather gloves and an old Broncos winter cap. Her hands reached for the gloves as a fresh wave of tears slid down her cheeks. "I don't want this." Her pleas were as weak as her will and would do no good.

Her fingers clutched a couple of stiff papers, and she brought them forth from the drawer bottom into the limited light of the hallway. Holding one in each hand, she noted the structure and template of each was the same. The content within each was different and they both had a different name on them. Each was titled the same though and the title alone brought forth a wave of nausea.

A gasp choked free of her and her hands shook with nervous energy as she scanned the two documents. An emotional outburst was building inside her and it wouldn't be denied.

Each stiff paper was titled **Death Certificate** and was comprised of a series of informational boxes.

On both papers were fields labeled, **Name of Decedent**. One was filled with the typed words - *Aaron Ettinger*, the other with *Jenna Ettinger*.

Each form had the same address on it, her home address, and each listed **Cause of Death** - *multiple traumatic injuries due to motor vehicle collision.*

"No!" Pam fell to her knees in the hallway. She knelt before the altar the antique table had become while crying over the two papers. "This isn't real!" She screeched and howled. "Someone make this stop!"

Coming Up Short 9

A sound from the living room pierced her veil of misery, and she tilted an ear in its direction. Coming to her from the living room was the sound of keys in the front door lock. The lock turned and the rattle of keys invaded her home.

"Aaron?" Pam stuffed the papers back into the drawer, shoved the black leather gloves over them again, and slid the drawer shut. She forced herself to her feet and dried her eyes with the sleeve of her blouse. "Aaron, Jenna, is that you?" She called out while stepping away from the table.

The familiar squeak of the front door opening fully echoed down the hall, followed by Aaron's happy voice. "Who else would it be?"

"Honey?" Pam's voice choked out the word and she ran down the hall. "Jenna?"

"Yeah, I'm here, mom. Dad picked me up because you forgot." Her daughter sounded pissy and Pam had never been happier to hear the irritated tone from her only child.

She scurried into the living room where Aaron and Jenna were plopping their things on the floor by the closed front door.

Without hesitation, Pam dodged furniture like an Olympic sprinter. She threw her arms around her family and clutched them close. Aaron hugged her back while Jenna tried to free herself from the death grip Pam had on her.

"Oh, thank God! It's you! I had the most awful

dream!" Pam cried.

"Geez, mom, let me go. First, you forget me and now this…" Jenna finally shrugged free.

Pam kissed Aaron on his cheek and separated herself from him as well. She took them in, each a little puzzled by her aggressive love. "I'm sorry I forgot you, honey. I don't know where my head is lately." The sight of them standing before her, each whole and healthy, was overwhelming. "I'm so grateful for each of you. Please be careful out there, okay? For me?"

"I think I recall this conversation from dinner, Mom." Jenna rolled her eyes, clearly uncomfortable with Pam's emotion. "We're fine."

Aaron angled his head at her and asked, "What happened in that dream of yours? Did we die or something?"

"No, nothing like that," Pam lied. "I'm just so happy you're both home."

★★★

After the rough interaction with Stella, Pam decided to leave her coworker and friend alone for the rest of the day. Now, back at work the next morning, she intentionally sought out Stella, finding her cleaning one of the patient intake interview rooms.

Approaching cautiously, she stood in the open doorway, and said, "Hi Stella. I'm sorry about what happened yesterday."

Coming Up Short 9

Stella pushed a table back into place in the center of the room and straightened while glancing at her. She offered Pam a large smile and a friendly wave. "Hi, Dr. Ettinger. Did you break something yesterday? I'm afraid I haven't discovered it yet if you have." She crossed the room, waiting for Pam to inform her of her misdeeds.

"Oh, no, nothing that I broke. I meant the interaction we had. I could have handled that better, I'm afraid." Pam half smiled. "And I'm sorry about it."

Stella stood in front of her, still in the room, and replied, "I guess I'm confused. What did we talk about yesterday?"

"The whole thing about you losing your mother...I showed you the file. Do you remember?" Pam frowned. Stella was either in far worse shape than she imagined, or Pam was having some cognitive issues of her own.

Stella's face changed. At first, her look of curiosity transitioned into concern. Now, the concern vanished in favor of empathy. Pam noted how Stella's right hand found the necklace under her shirt. She rubbed the small black stone as she replied, "I don't recall that conversation, Dr. Ettinger, and anyway, I never had a mother. She left when I was super young."

Stella's hand fell away from the necklace. She moved past Pam into the hall. Soon, she was out of sight. As Pam watched her disappear around a corner, she knew she needed to revisit Stella's patient file one more time. "Maybe it really is me who's losing her mind."

★★★

Coming Up Short 9

Pam stood in the past patient file room staring at Stella's file. Everything she'd read before was there, and now it was all coming together in her mind. "I missed it the first time." She was pissed at herself for her poor analytical skills. What she needed to know was right there in front of her the whole time.

Finally, she understood what had taken place to create such a change in Stella. The way she'd read Wilthrop's notes before, she thought he was performing two separate courses of treatment on Stella. One was some type of high-end drug therapy. The other was the sensory deprivation pool. His notes didn't lie. He had done those things, but they weren't two separate treatments, they were one.

He'd been drugging Stella before putting her in the pool. Every medication he'd used was some sort of depressant or relaxant. While his notes didn't specifically say he'd done this. It became obvious once she began digging into the details of the treatment. If Pam had to make a guess, she'd say Wilthrop was drugging Stella to keep her in the pool longer. "Disgusting."

"What's disgusting?"

Pam whirled around to find Wilthrop standing in the file room doorway. "Pam, you look like the child who got caught with her hand in the cookie jar."

Her hands began to shake, and the paper file rattled against her leg. "You did it, didn't you? You drugged Stella before putting her in the pool."

He stepped into the room, closer to her, and allowed the door to close behind him. His white lab coat flapped as he moved. He carried the appearance of a caped villain in a superhero movie. His eyebrows raised as he told her, "I'm on the verge of a substantial breakthrough and I won't allow anyone, including you, to mess it up for me." He held out a hand. "I'll take that."

She slapped the file onto his palm. "How long did you have her in the pool? You've caused her severe memory lapse. Some days, she recalls her mother, and others she doesn't, and I suspect she's become delusional regarding Paul."

"These things aren't your concern. She's not your patient." He tucked the file under his arm and stepped aside. "Your key will no longer work to this room. You've abused your privilege, and if it happens again, we'll need to discuss your employment at this facility."

"I'll go to the APA and the AMA about your unethical experimentation, if that's what it takes." Before he could further threaten her, Pam turned and exited the storage room.

★★★

The end of the day had arrived without further contact with Wilthrop. At first, Pam had been worried he would fire her, but she changed her mind. He would never dismiss her because she'd expose his unethical treatment of patients and employees. The exposure would end his career.

No, Wilthrop wasn't stupid. She wasn't on the cusp of the unemployment line.

Coming Up Short 9

Pam stood in the dark sensory deprivation pool room, alone, more than tempted to lie in its warm and relaxing waters for ten minutes. She could use the peace and clarity for her exhausted mind.

Next to her, on a table, was the loud timer they used to announce to patients it was time to get out of the pool. She set the digital timer for twelve minutes, kicked off her shoes, slipped out of her skirt and blouse, and moved to the edge of the pool. Light, soft, and blue around the edges of the room was the only illumination the room had to offer. The walls were covered in a thick foam batting, so the room was almost perfectly soundproof, and it was noticeable. The air had a heavy, dead weight to it.

Next to the steps into the pool, a small cabinet held the goggles and earplugs she'd need for the experience to do as was intended.

After fitting the goggles over her eyes, and the earplugs in, she dipped her toes into the water. It bathed her in warm comfort. Specifically, the water was maintained at a perfect 93.5 degrees Fahrenheit. This was the temperature that relaxed the body, and after a minute or so, created the sensation of no contact with anything.

Of course, the water was also thick with saline, set to a specific gravity solution of 1.27. It was this density that created the proper buoyancy needed to be weightless. The combination of temperature and density allowed people to float on the surface without fear of sinking.

Once she stepped fully into the water, which was only a little over three feet deep, she would notice the

Coming Up Short

viscosity of the water. And once she lay in it, she would discover the strange feel of a gravity-less universe. It would only take a minute to find peace and tranquility and for her mind to begin breaking down her current stressors. Pure relaxation was only a couple of footsteps away.

The air behind her back moved, tickling her bare flesh. The space was kept at temperature with radiant heat to prevent any sensation on the skin, which meant someone was in the room with her. Otherwise, there would be no shifting air currents.

Pam spun, panic gripping her, and found herself face to face with Dr. Wilthrop. He had sneaked up on her intentionally and the mischievous gleam in his eye was evidence of his cunning. He seldom appeared to be anything other than the professional expert she'd always known. The man who stood before her now was anything but professional. He was angry and his intentions weren't good. He was a monster.

She opened her mouth to scream as his right hand flashed forward and a stabbing pain radiated up her arm. He dropped a syringe to the pool deck and wrapped his arms around her as she began to fall.

"What did you…do…" Her words seemed to disband into individual letters and float away.

He'd drugged her. She knew this because of the warm feeling that spread from her left arm, across her chest, and into her head. Her eyes blinked shut, and she felt her worry and panic drift as if it rolled on gentle waves in ocean currents. The adrenaline in her system ebbed and her breathing slowed.

Coming Up Short 9

She couldn't hear Wilthrop or anything else. Whether this was due to the earplugs or the drug coursing through her, she wasn't sure. In all truth, it no longer mattered. She considered many random thoughts that she figured were common at the end of anyone's life. There was the regret she had over never making peace with her older brother before he passed away, and the many times she'd swatted away nice, caring men who wanted a relationship with her. Her career had always been the priority, and she'd ended up alone because of it. Having a child was always the thing she thought she'd eventually get to until she found herself over forty.

A family would have made her life so much better, so much richer, but she'd ignored that aspect in favor of status, success, and money. She regretted it, but now it was far too late.

In contrast to the sleepiness and drifting she felt, a pair of hands clutched her shoulders. They assaulted her out of the abyss in which she now lived. The suddenness of their grip brought a moan of displeasure from her. Another pair of hands clutched her legs, and she felt herself being lifted out of warmth and peace into cold air. She shivered and begged to be taken back to the warmth.

"Get the goggles off and don't forget the earplugs! For God's sake, how long has she been in there?" It was Wilthrop speaking to someone else.

"I don't know." A woman answered him.

She felt herself lifted free of the warm, loving womb she'd been tucked into and dropped onto a cold, hard surface. Her head was moved around, and

Coming Up Short 9

something was ripped free of her face. Her eyes were forced open, and a brutal light invaded them. She moaned again and tried to push away from the brightness.

"She's responsive." Dr. Wilthrop barked at the woman again. "Help me get her sitting up."

Pam's back was lifted by a pair of hands, and her body responded. Stomach muscles automatically clenched, and she sat up, gasping for air. Her eyes focused on the sensory deprivation pool beyond her feet. A trail of water across concrete linked her to the small body of water.

Her mind seemed to clear with the sensation of the hands on her back, and she spoke. "What happened?"

"The better question..." Wilthrop moved to stand in front of her. "Is, what were you thinking? You had to have been in there for over an hour." He was displeased. His tone was sharp and his words short.

"I...I..." Pam recalled coming to the pool to relax. "I needed to relax. I set the timer."

On her other side, Stella stepped forward. "The alarm isn't set. It's off, which is why someone on staff needs to know when anyone goes into the pool, including you."

Wilthrop said, "You were in the middle of a pretty good hallucination. If you'd gone much longer, you would have experienced some extensive memory loss."

Coming Up Short 9

Pam placed her hands on the sides of her head. "Do you mean…"

"Everything that has run through your head for the past hour is fiction. It was all hallucination." He stared down at her, his hands on his hips.

"None of that was real?" She sighed and asked Stella to help her to her feet.

"As you know, doctor, what you've done here is exceptionally dangerous." Wilthrop would be angry for weeks.

Pam stood on shaky legs with Stella's help. "I'm sorry. I thought I had the timer set."

Wilthrop turned away. "I have a patient session. I'll assume we won't need to have this discussion again, doctor." He stormed out of the poolroom.

Pam thought about the things she saw in her hallucination. "It was all so real."

Stella handed her a towel. "That's why I won't get in that thing."

"You were there, uh…" Pam forced her mind back into the dream. "You were reconnecting with an old boyfriend, Paul, and you couldn't seem to remember your mom…and you got a necklace in the mail. You were convinced it had the power to make everything alright in your life." Pam wiped herself down with the towel. "I told you it was strange."

Stella scowled. "That necklace. What did it look like?"

Pam shrugged into her top and skirt. "The chain was gold, and there was a stone. It was black and oval. To me, it looked like obsidian. I still can't believe it was all a hallucination. Shit, that's scary."

"Dr. Ettinger." Stella waited until Pam returned her gaze to continue speaking. "Did that necklace look like this?" She withdrew a gold chain with a dangling black stone at the bottom from inside her blue blouse.

Pam felt her mouth fall open. "You mean it's real?"

"So, this is it? This is the necklace you saw?" Stella asked again.

"Yes, that's it, exactly." She touched the gold chain hanging from Stella's hand.

"I got it in the mail. I don't know who sent it." Stell said.

Pam glanced from the jewelry to Stella. "Did you show me this before?"

"No, that's not possible."

"Why?"

Stella allowed the black stone to fall against her chest by releasing the necklace. "Because I just got it out of my mailbox today, and for the record, what you described about me feeling optimistic about the future when I wear it is true. It's exactly how it makes me feel, like there's hope, like I'm light and happy. When it's around my neck, I know good things are coming."

Pam stared into Stella's eyes despite the darkness in the room. "I have a question for you."

"Yeah?" Stella answered with a question of her own.

"Please tell me the truth about this, alright?" Pam watched Stella nod her head. She asked her question, though she was worried about the answer. "Was I ever married that you know? Did I have a family?"

The expression on Stella's face faltered into sadness. She broke eye contact by staring down at her hands. "Well, I know you want one for sure, but no, you're as single as I am." Stella turned away. "I need to get home now."

"Stella?" Pam called, but the woman was already out of the pool area and heading into the hallway.

Pam slipped into her pumps and followed the path Stella had taken to the exit. The hour in the pool had her feeling shaky and as if she couldn't recall important parts of her life. It was a strange thing to not know if she was single or married, and yet, no significant other came to mind. It was why she'd asked the question. The way Stella had reacted had her head spinning. Was Stella lying? Pam couldn't recall a husband or children, but a specific memory from her hallucination kept prodding her. It was something that would be easy to check, though, and that was the good news.

All she had to do was go home and check the drawer in the antique table in her hall.

★★★

The table stood, solitary in dim light, mocking her terror. The pervasive fear that clutched her was irrational, and she knew it. Still, she stood, afraid to do the thing that needed to be done. All it would take would be to grab the drawer handle and yank it open. It was a simple movement that would be over in a second, but the idea there could be documentation inside that would shatter her heart and mind was beyond terrifying.

"Please, don't be there..." she spoke, and the table ignored her. It had no desire to accommodate her. Whatever secrets it held were there to discover, regardless of her desires.

"Dammit!" Pam clutched the cold metal handle and slid the drawer open. She held pent-up breath in her chest and forced her eyes downward. A mass of folded gloves and winter hats were haphazardly stuffed into the tight space. She'd come this far. Now it was time to finish the job.

Pam plunged both hands into the drawer, feeling under the layers of winter accessories for the papers she recalled from her hallucination. She was either an idiot for having spent too long in the sensory deprivation pool, or she was absolutely losing her mind. There wasn't much room in between the two scenarios. They were close neighbors and owned property next to each other in her head.

Coming Up Short 9

Her cold fingers felt something thin and dry shift along the drawer bottom. She clutched at the edges of what was obviously paper and pulled it free of the drawer. In her hands were the two death certificates she recalled from her time in the pool. This meant that she had subconsciously known about the death of her husband and daughter all along, but had repressed the memory.

A little desperate, unhealthy snicker escaped her throat. The irony was more than she could bear. She'd thought it was Stella who was unstable, but it had been her all along. "I'm a mess. It's me. I hid Aaron and Jenna's deaths from myself so that I could forget." Her breath hitched in her chest and a single sob ushered free.

The rough corner of another piece of paper jutted from the drawer between a blue mitten and a black leather glove. This one, much thinner than the death certificates she held in her hands. Pam pulled it loose from the drawer and held it up in the light that came from her bedroom. An article from The Daily Register detailed the death of her husband and daughter.

She scanned the three-paragraph article, multiple sentences sticking in her psyche like an invading alien army. 'Tragic auto accident… deaths of Paul and Jenna Ettinger… father and daughter, both found deceased at the scene…survived by Dr. Pamela Ettinger, wife and mother…'

"They died in an accident. My family, they were mine and they're…gone." A sorrow-filled moan tore free of her. Her eyes, filled with spilling tears, checked the date at the top of the article. "Oh, my God." Pam read

Coming Up Short 9

the small date again. "It's been a month. I lost them a month ago."

Flashes of an overcast day permeated her head. She dropped the papers on the floor and staggered toward her bedroom. In her mind, she recalled an image of double caskets being lowered at the same time into the greedy, hungry earth. The soil had claimed her family, leaving her devastated and all alone. "It happened. It was all real, and I blocked it out, but how…how did I forget them for a month?"

She sat on the foot of her king-sized bed, her head in her hands, doing her best to force away the coming migraine. Her chest heaved with the sobs that racked her body, but she didn't notice. All she could do, all she could handle, was to replay the glimpses of their funeral in her head over and over. Her mind thirsted to understand what she'd done to abandon the memories of her love and her child. How had she operated a normal life without once discovering what she'd buried?

How had she made losing her family okay?

Her right hand rose to her throat to finger the cold, dark stone at the bottom of the gold chain around her neck. As her finger rubbed against the stone, her breathing slowed, and her tears dried.

Her head cleared, and she stared across the room at her open bedroom door. Somehow, she'd come home to sit on her bed. For what purpose, she wasn't sure, but here she was. While her right hand fondled the wonderful stone at the base of her slender throat, her left hand patted her cheeks dry with the sleeve of her blouse.

Coming Up Short 9

Thank God for the necklace. It had come to her out of the blue. She'd never known who thought enough of her to bestow the gift upon her, but she was eternally grateful.

A warm glow bloomed in her chest, replacing stress and tension. She sensed that she might have been contemplating something sad or upsetting, but those thoughts were long gone. Only an echo of unhappiness remained and even that was slinking away back into the dingy shadows from which it had come.

Pam sighed. Thank God for the necklace. It was her most treasured gift, despite not knowing where it had come from, and now she felt good. She was relaxed and ready for her evening.

If she had a spouse, she'd tell him all about her day and then settle in to watch a TV show together before going to bed. Of course, she'd do those things, but alone, since she'd never married or had children. She'd chosen a solitary life, but that was alright. It was her path to walk, and who knew? Maybe someday she would eventually meet someone.

The next day at work, after her patient sessions, she'd use the sensory deprivation pool for a few minutes to relax and reflect on her life. It would do her some good.

★★★

Stella Madison stood on the viewing side of the two-way mirror, staring into the sensory deprivation pool. There, naked, and fully exposed, floated Dr. Pamela Ettinger, unaware and oblivious of what was really happening to her. It tugged at Stella's heart to see such a wonderful woman suffer such tragedy. She touched the pile of Pam's clothing on the table beside her. On top was a small gold chain necklace with a beautiful black stone. Her eyes flicked from the jewelry to Dr. Wilthrop, who monitored Pam's vitals on a monitor.

Wilthrop was brilliant and was the only hope Pam had of recovering after the recent devastating events in her life. The poor woman's husband and child had died in a terrible accident and Pam had never recovered. It had been a month and Pam had only become more distant, more morose.

Though Stella could easily glance at the moving red digital numbers on the wall-mounted timer, Stella asked Wilthrop, "How long has she been in there now?"

"Eight hours and fifteen minutes." He answered without a hint of emotion.

Stella's fingers found the little black stone on Pam's necklace and she rubbed it between a finger and thumb. It was smooth and soothing to her frayed nerves. Eight hours was a long time. It was a long time to float in the mental void where Pam was, and it was a long time to be on the Benzodiazepine medication Wilthrop had given her. "I'm worried about her. Is she going to be okay?"

"Yes. She suffered severe psychosis after the tragic death of her family. A complete reset of her memories is the only way we can bring her back to who she was before the accident. Without this, she'll be lost forever and require institutionalization for the remainder of her life."

"It's such a shame." Stella sighed. She watched through the glass as Pam twitched in the pool. Little waves spread across the pool's surface before dying out. "She was a brilliant doctor who helped so many people, but in the end, she couldn't help herself."

Wilthrop replied, "She's lucky she was an employee here when all this happened. Hopefully, I can get her back to who she was before. Time will tell. This is the only chance of that happening. By the time we all recognized the signs of her illness, she was far too lost."

Stella lifted the necklace from Pam's skirt and held it up to sparkle under the fluorescent lighting. "This seems familiar to me. Have you ever seen me wearing anything like this? I feel like I once might have had a similar necklace, but I can't recall."

Wilthrop frowned at her. "No, I don't recall seeing you wearing anything like it."

"I wonder where she got it." Stella placed the piece of jewelry back on Pam's clothing but kept the black stone in her closed palm.

★★★

Dr. Wilthrop sat at his desk, thinking about his accomplishments in the field of selective memory dissolution. The process he'd invented using a combination of drug therapy, and sensory deprivation, was so advanced that once he presented his findings to the American Psychiatric Institute, he was certain to gain serious status among the elite in his profession, and he would most likely become a very wealthy man. His newfound treatment process selectively targeted the painful events in people's lives that caused them so much stress and poor health. The process was genius because it simply created a ripe environment for the mind to do what it was programmed to do; eliminate emotional pain.

It was the entire reason the subconscious existed, only the subconscious mind was flawed.

In most people, dribbles of painful memories came through the veil between the subconscious and conscious minds, thus creating all types of psychosis. This failure was accurately to blame for eating disorders, drinking, drug problems, and relationship issues.

He grinned to himself and swallowed the remainder of the bourbon in his Glencairn glass. It was but a small celebratory drink. Later, once home, he would do much better for himself. It wouldn't take too long for Pam to wake up and for him to determine the effectiveness of her treatment.

Another round in the pool was a possibility, but most of his patients had responded positively after one session. Pam was a friend and valued colleague. He wanted her back soon, working in the clinic. He needed someone to take on the more mundane caseload of phobias and stress disorders while he worked on his research, which was why he'd hired her from the onset.

The timing of the death of her husband and daughter wasn't great, but not impossible to overcome.

Coming Up Short 9

The phone on his desk rang once, and he retrieved it from its cradle. "Wilthrop."

"Dr. Wilthrop, it's Stella. Dr. Ettinger is waking."

He replied, "I'll be right there," and hung up the phone. It was time to evaluate Pam and determine if more time in the pool would be necessary.

As he stood, he reached out to shut one of his desk drawers. It was the small drawer in the top row. He stared down at the collection of cheap little gold necklaces with fake obsidian stones. Under the costume jewelry was a stack of cards, all with the same words on them.

Peace comes with forgiveness, but contentment comes with forgetting.

He'd written the line as a prelude to the advanced treatment he gave his memory-dissolution patients. Of course, while he planted the subconscious seeds about the power of the necklace, the patients were never aware of what he was doing. It was all based on them being placed in a semi-hypnotic state without their awareness. He did it casually, through mundane conversation.

He snapped the drawer closed and locked it with a key on the ring he kept in his pocket.

It was time to visit Pam.

★★★

Coming Up Short 9

"How're you feeling?" Stella asked.

Pam opened her eyes at the sound of Stella's voice. "Fuzzy."

"Do you know who I am?" Stella asked.

"Stella." Pam grimaced. "I'm not that far gone, but…"

"You poor thing." Stella stood at her bedside. "But what?"

Pam forced her eyes open wide and stared at Stella, "I don't remember a lot about you…don't you have a husband, or maybe we discussed your mother…something like that?"

"No, I don't have either," Stella said in a hushed voice.

The door to Pam's room opened and Dr. Wilthrop entered. "Stella, would you excuse us, please?" The doctor shot an intense stare at Stella and held the room door open for her.

"Sure." Stella, getting his hint, smiled and moved out of the room.

Pam focused on Wilthrop. "Dr. Wilthrop. What happened to me? I can't remember much. I feel all hazy and…lost."

Wilthrop pulled a chair up to her bed and sat. "You tripped in your office and hit your head on the corner of your desk. The welt is gone now, but you were out for a couple of days. I'm afraid you hit your head pretty hard. I was worried you may not regain consciousness. Fortunately, you were in the right place for optimal care, and I have to say, you're looking and sounding much better."

"Wow, I don't recall any of that," Pam admitted, reaching a hand up to feel her head.

"Yes, I should guess not, but you'll be fine. We'll keep you under observation for a couple more hours and then send you home." He smiled at her.

Pam tried sitting up. "Do you have my phone? I should call…"

"Who do you need to call?" Wilthrop eyed her carefully.

She searched her mind and shrugged. "That's weird, but no one. There is no one to call. I'm alone in the world."

Wilthrop patted her on the arm and stood. "Well, who knows? Maybe one day you'll meet someone special."

"I doubt it," Pam replied. "I'm not the marrying kind. I'll never have a family."

Coming Up Short 9

Coming Up Short 9

CHOICES

His arms were scratched and cut. They bled little rivers of red down toward his wrists.

Tyler glanced around the unfinished basement, unsure of how he'd gotten there. His breath came in ragged gasps. Sweat poured down his face and stung several places on his cheeks and nose. He had no mirror, but he figured his face looked a lot like his arms; shredded and raw. The sting of sweat in scratches came from several places on his face.

It reminded him of the time, as a little kid, that he'd gotten hot and sweaty riding his bike and then crashed, face-planting himself into a curb.

The pain told him something had happened, and it had happened recently. He wondered if his mother knew about it. She'd kill him if he'd gotten into a fight with the kid at the end of the block who was always flashing gang signs at him. The street gangs lived up to their reputation. They were a gang, a collective. They stuck together. If he hurt one of them, the rest would come after him and it wouldn't take long.

"Mom's going to be pissed." His mouth moved at an odd angle, and he knew it was because the left side of his cheek was swollen. It had happened before. The last time he'd gotten into a fight, he hadn't been able to chew for a week.

Coming Up Short 9

Maybe his mother was still at work. It was possible she knew nothing about what had happened.

"She's going to be so mad." He shivered. He'd been warned about his temper many times. Anger was his biggest enemy. He couldn't control it. The last time he'd busted some dumb kid's nose and arm in an alley in LoDo, he'd done it while he was blacked out. If it hadn't been for Shania, his girlfriend, pulling him away, he would have killed the kid and not even known it.

Tyler shivered at the thought of his mother coming home. There would be no way to hide his wounds. She was going to see him, eventually.

He glanced down at the front of his hoodie. He sat on a metal folding chair. A mixture of sweat and blood stained the hoodie and his crotch.

"What the hell happened?" He tried to wipe his hands on his jeans, but they were also slick with sweat. He reached lower and found dry spots in the fabric at the backs of his calves.

Something bad had happened, and he had no memory of it.

Another thought came into his head. "Shit!" He'd have to explain all his cuts and scrapes to Shania, too. If she saw them, she might think he was all violence and want to dump him. "That's all I freaking need."

She was the most beautiful girl he'd ever seen, and the idea she liked him as much as he liked her amazed him. From her deep green eyes, her black hair, pale skin, and curvy body, she was the perfect girl. She had transfixed him from the moment he'd met her.

"I can't mix her up in this." It wouldn't be right, and he didn't want to lose her over whatever he'd done.

His mind returned to the idea that his mother would be home soon. Not much in life created fear in his heart. The idea of his mother going ballistic put true terror in him, though. She was about all he feared in the world. She'd raised him on her own, and though he hated her deep in his heart, he had respect for her. Brenda looked like a typical thirty-eight-year-old working mom. She was a little overweight, which most people thought made her look sweet and kind.

It wasn't true, though, not at all. No one on the outside of their small home knew the truth about her, but the temper tantrums he had grown into, he had learned from her.

The two of them fought often. He was a sixteen-year-old kid trying to become a man, and it was hard to do under the watchful, intrusive eye of a domineering mother.

He recalled the many times he'd seen Brenda lose her shit. Anytime he was winning an argument with her, she would become violent to get him to shut up. He'd seen her clear off a kitchen counter with her arm in a sudden rage, sending food and dishes to shatter on the floor. One time, she punched a hole in the dining wall when he'd questioned her about their bills.

In his mind, he could see her angry, puffy red face. It was always the first sign she was going to erupt.

Coming Up Short 9

"Yeah, I learned it from you, Mom." He muttered.

His eyes trailed from his hands in his lap to the concrete floor under his feet. "Oh, shit!" That little funny feeling that he was about to get his ass kicked crawled into his stomach to stir his gut up into an acidic mess.

His eyes roamed the bloody trail on the basement floor and his mind solidified on the idea that he had blacked out and gotten into trouble. A sob choked out of him, and he pushed it back. He needed to find his self-preservation mode. Some shit had gone down and if he had seriously injured someone, he needed to cover his ass. Once Brenda saw him, she'd beat him. No doubt about it, she'd hurt him. Normally, that would be the worst thing that would happen, but if whoever he'd hurt called the cops…

"I'll go to fucking prison." His eyes followed the swaths of red fluid where they crossed the floor. Someone dragged a person through the basement, and that person bled profusely.

He sat up in his chair. "Dammit!" Trouble was coming for him. No doubt about it and he couldn't recall a shitting thing.

His eyes tracked the mess to the far wall where it ended at the freezer chest.

"Oh, no…"

The freezer, large and white, sat in the corner of the basement where it had been for years. In the past, his mother had used it for meat storage and packages of frozen veggies. She had always been paranoid about an emergency happening and wanted to be prepared for it. It was why, for so long, she had kept the large appliance so stocked full of food.

The various scenarios she decided were going to befall humanity at any moment included nuclear war, a biological agent of some sort that would poison most of the population, or potentially a virus that would have the world locked in their homes as governments fell.

When Covid happened, she'd warned him, "They're trying, Tyler. They're trying to thin the herd and we're a part of the group they want to thin."

Of course, all her frozen meal purchases had come to an end when he'd informed her that if an emergency came along in which they'd need to rely on their stores of food, it would almost certainly come with a loss of electrical power.

Tyler still remembered the argument they'd had that day. Their argument had been one of their more famous knock-down drag outs, and he'd been punished severely for his role. It had taken a week before he could fully open his right eye. The consequences had been worth it, though. The look on his mother's face, when she realized he was right, was everything he'd hoped it would be. Though he couldn't recall what he'd said to her, he remembered clearly the words she'd shouted back at him.

"You're a raving mad lunatic!" Her eyes had been so filled with venom that he'd laughed despite the pain he was in. Her words had never haunted him. His perspective on her hatred at that time was different. Despite being repeatedly hit in his face with her rolling pin, he had gotten to her and it had been magnificent.

Those types of victories were rare. He'd gotten his ass kicked for it, but he had won that small battle, and Brenda knew it.

It hadn't been easy being a teenager and navigating the storm that Brenda brought into his life. The dominance she held over him and his struggle against it was the central part of his existence since he had been a little kid. That he'd ended up a carbon copy of her, though, with his tendency to solve problems by lashing out with his fists, made him feel an awful combination of embarrassment and remorse.

He hated his mother, and yet, he had become her.

He had become a carbon copy of her, and the blood on him and across the basement floor was evidence.

His tear-stained eyes found their way up the side of the freezer. There was no mistaking the drops and smears of blood on it. They offered such stark contradiction to the white on the freezer that a blind man would have noticed them.

"God, almighty…what have I done?" His heart hammered away as though it desperately desired to escape him.

The sick thought in his head couldn't be escaped. He wanted to throw up. He wanted to fall from the chair and cry until the cops came to take him away for his crimes, but it wouldn't ever work out that way. He would never get off that easy because Brenda would find him long before the cops ever could, and once she saw her basement, once she looked inside the large freezer, he would die because she would kill him.

Plain and simple; dead. She'd tear one of his arms off and beat him to death with it.

Then she'd stuff his bleeding, swollen carcass into the…

"The freezer…just like I did to…"

He'd hurt someone badly, and if he'd put them in the freezer, it was because…

"Because I killed them…" His stomach rolled, and he bent over his knees, working hard to keep his breakfast inside him where it belonged. "I fucking killed someone, and it's your fault, Mother!"

A flash of an argument flipped end over end through his mind. He was upstairs in his house, in the kitchen. He had been screaming, and Brenda was there, but so was…

"Shania. She was there too."

His girlfriend had been with him when he had gotten into a monster fight with his mother.

"But why?"

Coming Up Short 9

Tyler racked his memory for the answers he sought, but he only got an image of an out-of-order sign. His mind had tried to hide whatever had happened from him, and if he couldn't get it back, he wouldn't know what to do.

A wicked voice from deep inside him spoke up to inform him he could always just get up and open the lid on the freezer.

Do it. It'll remind you real good, Ty, buddy. Then you'll know exactly what happened. You'll know precisely who you killed and stuffed into that freezer. You may doubt it, but you shouldn't. You even broke bones getting the body in there.

"Shut up!" He screamed into the basement. "I don't need you telling me what to do! I've had enough of that!"

Though he knew he was alone, it felt good to lash out at the intrusive voice in his head.

Geez, so sensitive. I'm only trying to help.

The voice fell silent, but only for a moment.

Hey! Maybe you finally gave that old bitch what she deserved…that'd be a real development, wouldn't it?

Tyler squeezed the sides of his head until he thought it would burst. Veins stood out on his forehead and his eyes bulged in their sockets. "Leave…me…the…HELL ALONE!"

Coming Up Short 9

The inside of his mind fell silent. An overhead lightbulb ticked in the heat it radiated. He slowed his breathing. He needed to recall what had happened. That Shania had been there when he and Brenda got into a fight was not good. Certainly, she wouldn't have stood by and let him hurt his mother.

A new thought occurred to him. "Maybe my head is making up the memory."

Maybe Shania had never been there to witness a major humiliation in his life. The way Brenda demeaned him, the way she hit him with anything she could get her hands on, was the most embarrassing aspect of his young life and the thing he fought hard to keep secret from everyone. It was such a shameful situation because once his mother became violent, he always backed down. Even when her fists, belt, shoe, or kitchen spoons rained blows down on him, he never raised a hand to her. He had not once through the years defended himself.

Not one time had he tried to return the favor, not once, and it wasn't because he was chivalrous or had a principle against hitting a woman. No, he had no respect or love for his mother. Tyler ducked and covered when the beatings came because she terrified him. He knew if he had ever raised a fist against her, she would kill him. He could run his mouth at her all he wanted, but when such an interaction resulted in her having a temper tantrum, he did his best to suffer the storm and later lick his wounds.

So, no, he would never have emasculated himself in front of Shania. The last thing he would have wanted was for her to see him and his mother fighting. Shania would have lost every ounce of respect she had for him if she had ever witnessed the way he cowered and pissed himself before his fist-swinging mother.

Again, the scene of Shania and Brenda blasted through his head. His mother's face radiating redness like a flashing emergency beacon in the night sky. Her body trembling with a rage she could no longer contain, her chubby face vibrating with hatred.

"She was about to go off..." He said to no one.

In his memory, Brenda opened her mouth and pointed at a visibly shaken and terrified Shania. "You're letting this whore ruin your life!"

Tyler clenched his eyes closed and whimpered. "Please..." he sobbed. "Make this stop."

Then go look in the freezer, you chickenshit.

The voice challenged him.

If you do that, it'll all go away.

"I can't." He answered. "I don't have it in me to see...to see..."

To see what you've done?

Tyler didn't answer. He didn't need to answer the question. Even a full-fledged, empty-headed idiot would see the truth in what his hidden voice said. He was scared. If he were to lift the freezer lid and stare into its frozen depths, what little remained of his sanity would shred. He would fall into the darkest pits of hell, never to return to the light of a sane day. That last little link to the present, to reality, would snap and an imagined world where no one but him existed would take over everything inside of him.

Brenda popped back into his mind. They stood in the kitchen. She held a tomato sauce-stained spoon. It rattled in her hand as she pointed it at Shania. "You're trying to trap him! How dare you, you little hussy!" Red sauce flew, staining the kitchen cabinets, but Brenda had no clue.

Trap you, huh?

"Trap me?" Tyler squirmed in his chair. He didn't want to know what the comment meant, but he knew. Deep down inside, he knew. His clenched gut insisted on it.

Oh, you know alright.

He rolled back in his chair and screamed at the ceiling. "NO! I don't know what it means!"

Ha! Yes, you do, chickenshit! Shania spilled the beans even though you warned her. Despite begging her not to, she confessed the dirty little secret you two had been carrying…

"NO! There was no secret!"

And the secret isn't the only thing she's carrying, is it, Ty, my man?

Coming Up Short 9

In his head, the scene in the kitchen returned. Shania was crying. Her tears streamed in slow motion, and he wished he could have wiped them away. He didn't like seeing her so hurt; so offended. She had placed a shaking hand on his arm, and said to Brenda, "We're happy together and we're having this baby, whether you like it or not!"

Tyler tilted off the folding chair to land on the cold basement concrete floor. "Oh, God no…"

Why does everyone always blame God? Tyler? Why are you blaming Him? HE didn't knock up Shania…it was you.

Brenda raised the spoon in her fist, her cherry red tomato head looking every bit like it would explode where it sat on her fat neck. "YOU DAMNED LITTLE WHORE!"

Tyler rolled on the basement floor. He perched himself on his knees and violently vomited as the memory expanded. His mother was swinging the metal spoon at Shania. He had no clue what to do…

Yes, you did. You knew exactly what to do. For the first time, you acted. Didn't you, Ty?

There was no use in trying to get the voice inside him to shut up. It would never be quiet. His guilty conscience would never relent, not for the rest of his life.

"Mother was out of control. She was going to have a heart attack…" He mumbled. "I had no choice."

Coming Up Short 9

You did, though. You had a choice, and you made it.

Inside the toxic memory, he reached behind him, finding the butcher knife Brenda had been using to cut up chicken. He grabbed it up, and he swung it forward.

His memory dropped away at the sound of the razor-sharp metal blade impaling human flesh. It slapped into meat with a sick squishing. The thud in his hand caused him to release the blade. A tinny sound echoed in his head.

"It was the knife hitting the kitchen tiles that made the sound. She pulled it free and dropped it to the floor." A wail erupted from him, and he staggered to his feet. "I can't take this anymore!" Across the room, the freezer stood alone, shimmering through a waterfall of tears.

You killed her, Ty. Her murder solved a few problems and created a few others, but the deed is done. Isn't it?

No longer hearing the wicked little voice from the shadows in his head, Tyler staggered forward. His mind conjured images of fists flying and a shrill voice screaming. Fists punched him, hands opened and closed involuntarily. Sharp nails scratched and clawed his arms and face. She had been caught off guard, but she wasn't without the ability to fight back.

Shaking the memory off, he stumbled forward. He needed to confirm what his memory had brought forth. He needed to know if it was true. If he had really killed her.

A step followed once more. Left, right, left, and right again. His feet moved until he stood before the freezer. The mess on its side was worse up close than it had been from across the basement. A substantial amount of blood crusted on it as a reminder of the violence he had perpetrated.

You got her good, Ty. Real good. Damn near sliced her kidney in half. The blood was everywhere. You remember, I know you do.

His hands found the underside of the indention in the freezer lid, and he lifted. Horror built inside him. A slice of memory returned, and though he wanted to deny what his mind shared with him; he couldn't push the mental images away.

The lid rose and his hands released it. His eyes followed it to the end of its upward arch, too afraid to see yet what nastiness awaited below in the freezer.

You came here for a reason, so look. Look at what you've done.

His hands fell away from the lid to rest at his sides. Sweat dripped from the end of his nose. It splashed on something very near the top of the freezer. Cool air rose to meet the heat of his fear. There was no hiding. He'd come to see, and he couldn't continue his avoidance for long. His eyes dropped.

"Oh, no…" For a moment, he feared someone had walked up to mourn his actions alongside him. It wasn't until the words stretched out into a long cry that he realized they came from him. "I didn't mean to…I'm so sorry…" The words choked their way free of him.

Of course you did. You knew what you were doing.

He stared down into a pair of gorgeous but dull green eyes. Dark hair cascaded down behind a pretty face like a filthy, frozen waterfall. Pale white skin with frost on the tip of a pert little nose greeted him with sadness and confusion.

"Why did I do it?"

Because you have never stood up to your mother and you never will.

"Shania, I'm so sorry…I, I'm so confused and…" the blood had finally stopped flowing but not before it had stained most of her dress. His eyes drifted higher, back to her neck. His handprints were there on her flesh, the bruises he'd given her staining her dark blue.

Are you devastated? Lost? Do you feel foolish? Stupid? You made a choice between them, Ty, and let's be honest. You were never going to not choose your mother. She terrifies you to the soul, but you have no ability to fight back, not now, or ever.

A squeak carried down the basement stairwell indicating the door to the first floor had opened. His body stiffened, and the hair on the back of his neck stood at attention. He knew it was coming, and he didn't have to wait long before his mother's voice called to him. "Tyler, quit your caterwauling and get that mess cleaned up! You're better off without that little hussy. She tried to trap you. Killing her was the only thing to do and no one will ever figure anything out as long as you clean up good. We'll take her upstairs tonight and get her into the trunk of the car so we can bury her in the woods. An animal will get to her soon enough and all evidence will be consumed by nature, just as God intended it." She waited for only a moment before calling out to him again. "Do you hear me, dammit? Answer me, boy!"

As though an electric cattle prod had been jammed up his ass, he screamed, "Yes, ma'am!"

"Then hurry up. Dinner's ready!" She slammed the basement door.

He lowered his voice and whispered, "I hate you, mother."

Yeah, but you'll never do anything about it.

"I hate her." His voice trembled with thick emotion as he lowered the freezer lid. "I could kill her."

Then go do it, crybaby. Why are you going to allow what happened to Shania to go unpunished? Besides, mother is an older woman now. She can't match your physical strength.

"Yes, you're right."

You could use the knife. She'll never see it coming, but you'll have to finally find some bravery to pull it off. Can you be brave, Ty?

Coming Up Short 9

"Yes, I can be brave." His mind was a whirling mess of anger and retribution.

Just go upstairs and do what you did before, but this time do it to her like you should have to start with, idiot.

Tyler turned away from the freezer and walked across the basement to the bottom of the stairs. He stared up at the crack of light that came from the bottom of the door. "Mother!" he screamed. "I don't think I'm scared of you anymore!"

The door opened and Brenda stared down at him. A tire iron in her hand tapped against the side of her leg as she spoke. She narrowed her eyes behind dark-framed glasses. "Well, you'd better damn well be scared, or you can get your skinny ass up here and show Mamma what a big man you are suddenly!" Her raspy voice challenged him. It dared him to confront her. It pleaded with him to come bring her some more light work. "Well? You coming up for a whoopin, or are you going to grow something between those damned ears besides a craving for a woman's body and get to work on that mess?" She stood waiting like a prison guard, daring a felon to attempt an escape. She watched the fight seep out of him and rolled her eyes. "That's what I thought. Get to work."

Tyler's shoulders sunk and he turned away from the stairs. "Yes, ma'am."

What a pathetic loser you are...

The voice chided him. He had no fight left. Arguing about it was a waste of time. She'd crack him over the head with the iron the moment he came up the stairs if he didn't clean up and do as she'd instructed.

Go then! Do her bidding! You'll never escape her and the beatings, and you'll never have another girlfriend.

Behind him, on the stairs, a mop came crashing down, along with a couple of damp rags and a bottle of bathroom cleaner. Brenda called out, "Do it right, or I swear to God I'll make sure you don't have the equipment to knock up another woman. You hear?"

"Yes, ma'am."

… Coming Up Short 9

THROUGH THE GREEN GLASSES

"Is he having a good day today?" Andre asked Dr. Williams as he stared through the small glass window in the door. In the patient room, his grandfather sat in his recliner watching a baseball game that didn't seem to have captured his attention.

Dr. Williams glanced into the room, his bald head reflecting the hall's overhead fluorescent lights. The wire-framed glasses perched on his nose were exactly the type Andre would anticipate a doctor of psychiatry wearing. Dr. Williams sighed, "As you know, Huntington's disease can be a little random symptomatically. Yesterday, he seemed as clear as a bell, and even his tremors were largely absent. Today, he's had some lucid moments, but the disease continues to progress, Mr. Lujan. As you know, Huntington's is a type of dementia. He has good days and bad days. We'll continue to take good care of him." He snapped his fingers and turned his attention back to Andre. "I wanted to mention the new medication seems to be helping, and we've only had him on it for a few days."

"Alright, that's good to hear, at least." He thanked the doctor and opened the room door. He entered the room, shut the door behind him, and moved into a chair across from his grandfather.

Coming Up Short 9

The man sitting across from him meant the world to him. The diagnosis of Huntington's disease had probably hit him harder than anyone in his family. Even his mother, who was upset, wasn't as impacted. Of course, her way of dealing with the changes in her father was to stay away and live in denial. Her approach irritated Andre, but there was already enough stress, so he kept his mouth shut.

Unlike his mother, he tried to be realistic about his grandfather's diagnosis and prognosis. "Hey, Grandpa. How's it going today?"

Without moving his tired gray eyes away from the TV, the old man asked him, "Is the doctor still at the door?"

"No, he's gone."

Abe Lujan pivoted his gray head toward his grandson. His tired eyes were a reflection of how the disease had impacted him. At times, Andre was partially grateful that the old man didn't remember much from day to day. At other times, he felt guilty for seeing anything positive about what his grandpa was going through.

His grandpa asked, "You sure about that, Al?"

"Yeah, but I'm not…"

"You're not what?"

Coming Up Short 9

He wanted to say that he was Andre, Abe's grandson, and not Al, who was the old man's former business partner, but he let it go. It wasn't worth correcting. His grandpa would only return to calling him Al within a few minutes. It's how it always worked. Andre stared into his grandfather's waiting eyes. "Never mind." Al, the old man's former business partner, had died many years before, but he could play along for a while. Most likely, before his visit was over, his grandpa would call him someone else anyway.

"Okay, good. Listen…" Abe lowered his voice. "We need to be discreet about this, so no messing around."

The old man was on a roll today, it seemed. Andre simply agreed with him. It was what he usually did to get him to settle down. "Okay."

"There isn't much time. They know it's still out there and they'll do anything to get it." The old man shook his head. "We can't have that, or we're all done for." He held up a finger, hushing Andre. "You've got to go move it, Al, and never tell me where you put it. I'm afraid of what I might have already told them when I'm not entirely myself."

The urgency in Abe's voice caused Andre to sit up in the chair. "Uh, Grandpa, what are you talking about?"

Coming Up Short 9

"They're poisoning my mind, Al. I don't know for sure what I've told them. It scares me to death because if they find it, they'll be unstoppable, and they know it." The old man's voice was low, but stern and alive.

"I'm lost. I don't understand what we're talking about." Andre searched his grandfather's face and wondered if he should try to find Dr. Williams or one of the nurses. His grandpa seemed genuinely concerned, even frightened.

Abe clutched his arm and squeezed. For an old man, he was still plenty strong. His grip hurt, but Andre made no effort to move away. Abe spoke, "Get the glasses so you can use them and get the blade. It's the only way, and they know it."

Andre swallowed though his mouth had gone dry. "Use them for what?"

"They'll be here soon. There isn't much time. Do you understand?" Abe asked, his eyes imploring Andre to move.

"These glasses. Where are they?" He asked the question because he felt like he had to, or his grandpa wouldn't relent.

Abe leaned closer to him. "Under the floor. You know, out there…"

Coming Up Short 9

"Out where?"

The room door opened and the busy sounds of the hallway invaded Abe's small apartment sanctuary. A female nurse with brown hair and a smooth complexion smiled at them. "Is everything alright?" Her eyes switched back and forth between them before falling on Abe's grasp of Andre.

Abe released him and leaned back in his chair. "Yeah, we're good. What's it to you? Nosey busy body. Ain't no one got an ounce of privacy around here. These bastards come and go as they please, Al." Abe sighed and tapped a finger on his thigh. "It's like being in prison."

The nurse entered the room with a shrug and a grin at Andre. Without saying a word, she conveyed she was accustomed to Abe's verbal abuse. "Oh, Abe, you know I'm here to help you." She moved to the side of the old man's bed and placed a cup of water on his table and a syringe next to it. "I have the medication that Dr. Willimas ordered. This should help you feel better."

While her back was turned, Abe whispered to Andre, "Under the floor…way out there. Go get it." He nodded once and then raised his voice. "You people are a rude bunch of sons of bitches. I know that much for sure."

***

Coming Up Short 9

The drive to his two-bedroom apartment didn't take long, but on the way, Andre decided it was a good idea to check in with his mother. He alone couldn't handle all the visits his grandfather needed, so it was about time for her to do her share.

He dialed the number from the screen on his car dashboard and waited through three ring tones before she picked up. "Hello? Andre? Is everything alright?" It was her worried mother's tone, which was mostly fake. Charlotte Lujan worried only about herself.

"Yeah, it's okay. I went to see Grandpa," he said, sounding a little dourer than he desired.

"Awe, I'm sorry, honey." She said.

He wanted to hold back his feelings about her, but it was impossible. Since his father had died, his mom had done more and more retreating from life. She led a frivolous existence that included more partying than anyone her age had any right to do. She tried to dress like she was half her age and flirt with much younger men. It was embarrassing. More than once a friend had called to tell him they'd seen Charlotte Lujan in a bar. Usually, his friend would proclaim what a party beast she was and laugh about how inebriated she'd been. The situation had become humiliating to him, but his feelings would never deter her
behavior.

Coming Up Short 9

Andre spoke to her while guiding his car around a corner. "If you were sorry, you'd do something about it, like to go see him once in a while."

"What does that mean?" She whined her words in a way that made him cringe.

"It means you should go see your own father more often than you do. He's lonely and I don't blame him. The nursing home is stale and boring. The nurses and doctors barge into his space without knocking." He frowned, recalling how the last nurse had invaded his grandpa's sanctuary. "He has little privacy, and I can tell it's slowly killing him."

She paused before saying, "I go as much as my work schedule allows and…"

"No!" His voice raised. He couldn't help it. "You go as much as your partying lifestyle will allow you, which is next to never!"

"Dre! You watch how you speak to your mother! I demand you respect me!" Her voice quivered, and he knew that little telltale of emotion was her guilt speaking up. Once she became defensive, her next step was always tears.

"Never mind, mother." He was sorry he'd bothered to call her.

Coming Up Short 9

She returned to her whiny voice. "Now, don't be mad at me, Dre. You know I'm…"

He cut her off. There was no need to listen to her excuse-making. He'd heard it all before. "Grandpa told me to get something, but he said it's out there. Any idea what he meant by that? What did he mean when he said, out there?"

Charlotte replied, and he could almost see her eyes roll despite their invisible connection. "That old man remembers his cabin, but there's not much of it left any longer."

"Cabin?"

She answered, "Yeah, it was his retreat back in the day. Mom and I were never allowed to go there with him, so I was only out there a handful of times."

"Wow." Andre thought he knew everything there was to know about his grandpa's life. Hearing about the old property was interesting. "Where's this place at?"

"Oh, it doesn't matter. It's half falling apart and unsafe," she muttered. He guessed she was already drinking. Her voice wasn't mushy with slurred words yet, but it was coming.

"Still, where is it?" He pressed her, knowing how much she hated it when he wouldn't let something go.

"If you're insistent on knowing where it's at, it's out in the woods off Highway 7. You have to go out seven until the farmer's market, and then turn right. From there, you need to find an old gravel drive off that road. It's on the right about two miles up, but that driveway might have grown over by now. It's been years, Dre. Now, don't go running out there looking for ghosts. There aren't any there. It's just a crumbling old structure and your grandpa wouldn't want you out there messing around."

He didn't tell her that's exactly what his grandfather wanted. Instead, he informed her he was home, although the apartment complex was two blocks away still. He hung up with promises of stopping by on the weekend, which he wouldn't do. He'd only been on the phone with her for three minutes and it was already too much.

★★★

Andre stood on the side of the two-lane road that branched off route seven like his mother said. His car idled on the shoulder with the hazards blinking. He'd driven back and forth five times on the little stretch of road seeking the gravel drive his mother told him about. She had said it was probably grown over, and that much had to be true. The thick shrubs and grasses at the edge of the road on both sides were wild and untamed. There wasn't a house or business within five miles of the little stretch of road.

Once his grandfather stopped coming out to his cabin retreat, Mother Nature had taken over and sealed off the access to it.

He scanned the opposite side of the road and then diverted his attention to the thick woods next to him. Within a few feet of the road, towering pines, aspen, and oak trees crowded together as though they were protecting the greatest secret the world had never seen.

"Where are you?" He muttered as he walked along the edge of the road. He could work his way up and down the road all day and not see another car. It was a lonely stretch of the state and one that kids in high school had said was haunted. Of course, most smaller towns had such places. He had never bought into the hype or the rumors as a kid, although, if the woods were haunted, at least they weren't trying to lure unsuspecting people into their lair. If anything, they wanted humanity to stay away.

Andre moved along, past his car, to a slight indentation he hadn't noticed from the road. Here, the shoulder of the asphalt highway gave way to dirt and loose rock.

Coming Up Short 9

Rising on tiptoes, he peered over a wall of evergreen bush branches and hanging vine. Through the vegetation, a narrow lane wound past an old maple tree and disappeared.

He grinned. "Wow! You were closer than I knew all along."

After returning to his car to turn it off and lock it up, he pressed into the foliage and scraped his way through until he broke free of the green barrier and stood on a narrow dirt road.

Clearly, at one time, the road had been a little wider. Now, to drive on it would mean driving on the grasses and weeds that had overtaken most of the lane.

"Okay, now how far back is the cabin?" He stared into the forest, losing sight of the dirt road as it curled away to the left. The woods consumed it, and he hoped he would fare much better. The ominous feeling inside him was extinguished by a slight breeze. He needed to get rid of the negative vibe he'd had since leaving his car. The afternoon sun was on its farewell drop for the day, giving him only another hour or so of light. "Better get moving."

He stepped forward and plunged into the dimming day.

★★★

Coming Up Short 9

The dirt lane snaked through the woods much further than he thought possible. A retreating sun was enough to make him wonder if he should consider returning to the skinny path the next day, but as he considered a possible retreat, the trail rose a few feet and dead-ended in a small circle before what had to have been his grandfather's cabin.

The structure was old and clearly had been in much better shape once upon a time. On the other hand, it wasn't as dilapidated as Charlotte had indicated.

Wood-sided walls that appeared to have been white in the past were now grayed by the years that had passed. A covered porch ran the width of the structure, and under it was a door and two windows. The door, though solid, sat partially askew.

Andre stepped onto the porch. He ignored its creaks and groans of protest and approached the door. With a light push, it swung open. The dust living within the old structure wafted to him with the movement of the door. He stood still, staring inside, on the threshold of a sneeze attack.

Once the feeling passed, he stepped into the cabin and glanced around. On his right was an eat-in kitchen. The floor was largely covered in leaves that had blown in through the open front door.

The L-shaped cabinets on the walls reminded him of roughing it at the YMCA's cabins in his youth. A deep sink, originally white, was stained with rusty mineral streaks. Layers of dust covered everything inside the place, including an old sofa and chair which sat in the living room on his left. They faced a beautiful fireplace, which he thought was refreshing. Today, if anyone lived in the old place, there would be a sixty-inch TV hanging somewhere, distracting from the beauty of the stone fireplace.

"Nice place, Grandpa." A deep part of him was envious of any family member who had ever been allowed to come to the place with his grandpa. He couldn't blame the old man for keeping Charlotte away, though. She would have ruined the peaceful atmosphere regardless of her age.

Stepping fully inside, Andre focused on the job at hand. He was to look for something of importance to the old man, and no matter how illogical it seemed, the idea he could return them to the old man pleased him immensely.

Under the floor...way out there...

"Glasses and a blade. Weird." Andre moved toward the kitchen and with each step, bounced on the balls of his feet a little, testing for a loose floorboard.

His grandfather had hidden a couple of things of value. Maybe not monetary value, but at least of sentimental importance, and that was good enough for him.

Coming Up Short 9

Despite the growing shadows in the room, the result of a fading sun, he would walk all over the cabin floor until he found what he was after. Assuming, of course, the existence of the glasses and blade was more tangible than the creativity of a Huntington's riddled mind. It could be they were nothing more than a figment of Abe Lujan's fancy.

He progressed into the kitchen and eating area, working in an endless pattern of stepping on every square inch of the floor until he became certain he was in the wrong room. At the back of a little hall off the living room, he noticed a couple of doors. These had to be bedrooms, but before moving that far back into the shadows, he decided to check the living room. If the glasses and blade were of importance, and he was his grandfather, he would have stashed them somewhere that would be easy to access in a hurry.

That meant they were more likely to be in the front of the cabin than in one of the bedrooms. The bedrooms were for sleeping. The front of the cabin was all about being awake and alive. His grandpa had always been an active man who saw resting and sleep as a burdensome necessity. Abe saw sleep as a waste of hours when he could have been outside building something with his hands or reading a new novel by one of his favorite authors.

Andre moved back and forth across the living room in the same pattern as he had in the kitchen. It occurred to him that maybe he wouldn't find his

Coming Up Short

grandfather's secret stash. It might be the hidden pocket inside the floor would require tools to open. He hadn't thought of that before leaving his apartment, which made him feel stupid.

"Damn." He arrived in front of the fireplace and stared at the massive stone column and hearth. It hadn't been used in many years, and a part of him wanted to find some dead tree branches he could burn. He could spend the night in the old cabin with a fire burning, which would give him an extended amount of time to do his searching. It was unrealistic and wouldn't happen, but maybe someday his grandpa would allow him to use the old place.

Even without a hidden treasure, it represented a place of peace and solitude. He could come out, turn off his phone, cook a simple dinner, and then fall asleep in front of the fireplace, watching as the flames reached for the heavens. He snapped out of his wishful thinking and glanced around the open room.

Maybe a search of the bedroom floors was in order. Daylight had almost abandoned him, but he still had enough light to conduct a quick search.

Feeling disappointed, and a little exasperated, Andre plopped onto the hearth to rest and think. As he sat, one of the stones that comprised the raised platform shifted under him.

Coming Up Short 9

"What's this?" He stood again and stared down at the place where he'd been sitting. A flat piece of stone had slipped slightly to the right from where it had been. The increased gap between the large pieces of slate was obvious only if you were looking for something.

Grabbing it by the edge, he used leverage to push it further aside. The stone moved easily enough. He stopped shoving the flat chunk of rock and stared down into a dark crevice. From the limited light pouring into the living room through a window at the front of the cabin, he saw a large velvet bag stuffed into the gap between floor joists.

"I'll be lucky if I don't get bitten by a black widow or brown recluse." Why the poison spiders all were named with darker colors, he didn't know, but the eight-legged creatures had always freaked him out. He shivered while rolling up his sleeve. "Okay, here goes nothing."

Andre reached in quickly and plucked the black bag free of its hole. He set it on the hearth and shoved the large slate back into place to cover it up. In his mind, a whole legion of poisonous spiders was on the verge of escaping the cavity, and the only way to save himself was to lock them inside before they could make their escape.

With the stone in place, he inspected the bag for creepy crawlers. Feeling satisfied the bag was only a bag, he undid the drawstring at the top and pulled it open. Inside the black bag was darkness. There was no way he would risk reaching into the bag, so this time, he tilted the bag down and wiggled it until its contents came free to rest on the hearth.

"I'll be damned." He stared down at a pair of glasses with green-tinted lenses and a wood-handled knife of six inches. The knife blade gleamed in the light as though it were brand new. His eyes found an inscription carved into it.

"Monstrum interfectorem." He picked up the knife and felt its weight in the palm of his hand. It weighed more than seemed possible. The language on the handle seemed to be Latin, but who knew what the two words meant? "I need to look that up."

He placed the knife back on the hearth and retrieved the glasses. They were obviously old. The lenses needed polishing but appeared to be scratch-free. The arms were dual-banded and made of metal. He applied a slight pressure to one of the arms. It held steady, as though it was indestructible. The lenses were narrow and rectangular. They ran wide from side to side. Though the glasses were old, their design was modern, and way ahead of its time. "Jesus, how old are these things?"

He slipped the glasses up his nose and over his ears. "That's funny." The green tint of the lenses wasn't apparent in his sight. They also did nothing to make his vision any clearer or fuzzy. The world looked the same as it always had. "Wonder what the old man used this stuff for?"

Outside the cabin, a voice, male and gruff, wafted in through the open front door.

Andre crept to the side of the living room window to peek into the yard beyond the cabin. The layer of grime on the glass helped to obscure him as he lowered the green glasses on his nose to stare out into the fading day.

At first, he saw nothing that would explain the voice he heard, and he briefly contemplated the idea that the cabin was haunted. Before he could turn back to inspect the rooms behind him, a shrub at the side of the front yard shook. A few leaves fell to the earth as the large bush separated. From the center of the plant came a bull of a man. His bald head stuck out the top of a black suit. Only a white shirt made his black tie discernable. He wore dark glasses on his face and a small goatee on his chin.

"What's he doing out here?" Andre mumbled.

Behind the man, another massive form exited the same shrub. A branch tore free of the plant and fell to the ground, only to be stepped on by the second man to step free of the forest. Like the first man, he was bald and dressed in a black suit.

Coming Up Short 9

"They're twins." A feeling deep inside told him something was wrong with the two men who had come through the forest to reach the cabin. It also informed him the two men hadn't marched through the woods to share tea and biscuits. "What the hell is going on?"

As Andre stood watching, the second man stepped next to the first. Together, they stared at the cabin. The first one said something to the second, eliciting a slight nod.

From the back of his mind came his grandfather's voice. Loud and clear, the old man had been trying to get his attention.

They'll be here soon. There isn't much time. Do you understand?

"He was warning me." Chills crept up his spine as he thought about his grandpa sitting in the nursing home. "It's not a coincidence that these two are here."

Get the glasses so you can use them...

Andre slid the green-lensed glasses up his nose and stared at the two men. As his eyes locked onto them, he took a reflexive step backward. "Oh, my God. What are they?"

While the rest of the late afternoon appeared as it had only moments before, the two men had changed drastically. They were still twins, but no longer human.

Coming Up Short 9

Each still wore their suits, but that was where the similarities came to an abrupt end.

The men's faces had become ghostly white. An orange glow, like burning coals inside their heads, shone through jagged tears in their faces. The skin on their cheeks appeared to have been ripped in long streaks through which bright heat rippled. Behind their dark glasses, red eyes burned like far away brake lights on a highway. Wafting entrails of dark mists lingered around their bodies to lick at the air around the men. Whether because of the heat or their flickering toxic auras, the air seemed to ripple in their presence.

"This can't be." Andre slid the glasses off his face. The two bald human men that he'd seen before were back. Each of them stepped forward. They were still talking, planning their assault.

He pushed the green glasses back up his nose.

The air pulsed around the two monsters. Their red eyes searched the cabin, and the orange flames burned inside their heads.

A certain knowledge came to Andre in multiple parts.

He needed to get out and run. He needed to get back to his car and drive away from the old cabin as fast as possible. If he didn't, the two creatures, or whatever they were, would eat him alive and destroy his soul. That such beings could exist in reality was an affront to everything he had ever believed about his world and what he thought was possible.

There were monsters on the planet and every little child who ever believed the boogie man hid under their bed in the dark of night should forever be taken seriously.

The men had crossed half the distance to the cabin door and Andre recognized if there was no way out of the back of the cabin; he was in deep shit.

Turning away from the window, he tucked the glasses and knife deep into a front jeans pocket and hurried to the small hall on the other side of the room. Though the hall was dark and filled with mystery, it was preferable to the beasts coming for him.

Scurrying to the first door on his left, Andre yanked it open and hurried into a small bedroom. The skeletal remains of a bedframe sat against a far wall. Its only company in the room was an old dresser that was in as poor a shape as the cabin itself. Each of its drawers hung partially out of it, like loose teeth falling free of a large mouth.

Andre ignored the antiquated furnishings and eased the door closed behind him before crossing to the room's only window. Halfway up the single hung window was a slide lock. Andre grabbed it and twisted it

Coming Up Short 9

with his fingers. Paint residue held the lock in place like super glue.

"Dammit!" He swore under his breath.

From the front of the cabin, floorboards squeaked. There would be no retreating from the room for his escape. He would either get the window to slide open, or he'd bust the glass out of the frame. Either way, he intended to leave the room and run far away from the twin monsters who pursued him.

"Open!" He willed the glass as he used both hands on the stuck lock.

"He's been here…" A voice floated across the cabin, through the door, and into the bedroom.

The two men were out there, and they had come for him. They knew of his presence. It was only a matter of seconds before they would reach the bedroom.

Andre doubled his efforts on the lock. His fingers pulled on it until they turned white. It finally busted loose of the paint holding it in place. He released the turned lock and placed both his hands under the center of the window frame. He pushed upward, hard, as though he was in the weight room and doing one-hundred-pound military presses. The window rose faster than he expected with his exertion. As it climbed its rails, the old frame squealed in protest.

Coming Up Short 9

The footsteps in the living room paused, and the cabin fell into silence.

"Shit!" Andre tossed himself through the window opening, landed on his right side, and rolled through a pile of leaves and twigs. Without waiting to see if one of the creatures would pursue him, he jumped to his feet and hurried into the woods surrounding the cabin. He hurdled a large boulder, darted between two large trees, and pumped his legs until he had reached the dirt road at the front of the cabin.

Hiding behind a massive pine, he paused to catch his breath. The moment presented an opportunity to check the cabin front. He parted the branches that tickled his cheek and stared forward.

From the covered front porch, the two men stared back. Their eyes, behind dark sunglasses, searched the forest.

"Screw this!" Andre sprinted under the cover of massive trees to the path and didn't stop running until he was back in his car.

As he pulled onto the highway, he noticed a black SUV parked on the other side of the highway. It was undoubtedly the vehicle the two men, creatures, used to find the cabin. His car parked on the side of the road had probably helped them significantly. In the future, he'd need to be much more careful.

Coming Up Short 9

He stepped on the gas pedal harder and rocketed down the highway. Whatever amount of distance he could get from the two monsters would never be enough. His mind pulled up an image of how the two men appeared through the green lenses of his grandpa's glasses. The way the haunted light emanated through their skin terrified him.

He had no way to define them. They were an outlier of the darkest kind of anomalies. He'd never seen anything like them and hoped he never would again. His sentiments and revulsion alone wouldn't keep him safe, though. He needed to inform himself, and the only way he knew to do that was to reach his grandpa. If he hurried, he could make it before visiting hours ended at the nursing home. Hopefully, the old man would have it together enough to help him understand what he'd seen through the green glasses.

★★★

"Grandpa, can you hear me?" Andre sat in a chair next to his grandpa's bed.

Abe lay in the bed, his eyes blinking against the overhead lights. "I'm tired, kid. I need my rest."

"Right, and I'll let you in a minute, but…" Andre checked the door to the hall. It was still closed, as he had left it when he'd entered. "But I need to know about the green glasses and the blade. I got them, but there were these, uh, these…"

Coming Up Short 9

His grandfather's eyes blinked closed.

"Grandpa?" Andre placed a hand on his grandfather's arm. The old man didn't respond. "Grandpa? Can you just stay awake for another second?"

The door to the room opened, and Andre released Abe's arm. He glanced back to see Dr. Williams lean into the room.

"Hey, doc."

"Hi, Andre. I saw you through the window and thought I'd let you know visiting hours are over." He tapped the watch on his wrist. "Your grandfather had a big day. Come back and see him tomorrow. I know he loves your visits."

Andre stood. He glanced back at his grandpa, who slept soundlessly. "Sure thing."

★★★

"Hi, Dre." Arden, his gorgeous and scantily dressed roommate, greeted him upon entering their apartment. She stood before the refrigerator in a pair of short shorts and a button-up shirt with her long brown hair in a ponytail. As she said hello, she scanned the fridge for an evening snack.

"Hi," he said as he kicked off his shoes and stepped into the kitchen.

Coming Up Short 9

Arden extracted herself from the fridge and pushed the door closed. "Ever notice we never have anything good to eat here?"

"Yeah, I…" Andre turned away from her, afraid to take in her beauty for too long. She had no clue he had a giant-sized case of the hots for her and didn't want her to know. She was way out of his league, which only made his sentiments for her feel worse. He'd never have the relationship with Arden he desired, so getting too close to her was not a good idea. Living with her was a constant torture he couldn't imagine going without. They'd only been roommates, having met through a mutual friend, for three months and he wished she'd stay with him for another three years, at the least.

"Hey. You look a little lost." She reached for his arm and turned him back to face her. "It's easier to have a conversation if you look at the person talking to you." She grinned and another part of his heart melted. Her smile was the kind that could get a man in a lot of trouble. Nations had gone to war over less.

"Sorry, I wasn't trying to be rude." He reached into his pants pocket and withdrew the pair of glasses. "Ever seen anything like these?"

"Wow, those look old. Where'd you get them?" she asked while looking the green lenses over.

"My grandpa." He said, unsure whether saying much more was a good idea. He liked Arden. The last thing he wanted to do was involve her in whatever had happened, or almost happened, at the cabin. He stuffed the glasses back in his pocket and decided not to show her the knife.

"Are they a family heirloom or something?"

"I'm not sure." He admitted. "I had tried them on earlier, but they made me, uh…"

"You're not supposed to wear other people's glasses. That'll mess up your eyes." She informed him with a roll of her eyes and a smile.

He laughed. "Now you tell me."

"How's your grandpa doing?"

Andre considered his visit with the old man. "The same. He has good and shitty moments."

"Yeah, I remember when my grandma was suffering from Alzheimer's. It was rough. I'm sorry you're going through that. I know it was hard on me." She held out her hand. "Want me to clean up those glasses for you?"

"Oh, no. That's okay." He smiled. "I'm going to take them back to him tomorrow. He probably will have forgotten he gave them to me today." Andre didn't like lying to her about how he had come to find the glasses and knife, but the real story was rather unbelievable. He was even beginning to doubt what he'd seen at the cabin.

"I see." She stepped close to him and leaned up on her toes. He froze as she placed a gentle kiss on his cheek. "You looked like you needed that." She giggled.

"I did." He agreed.

She winked at him and returned to her bedroom.

For the second time that day, he was both perplexed and amazed.

★★★

"Put those away before they come in here and see them!" Abe hissed from his chair. "They're everywhere and they're going to kill me if they find those glasses and that blade. You know better than that, Al." Abe admonished Andre for exposing the glasses to the light of day. A strange look came over his face. "Wait…"

Andre was grateful for his grandpa's mental clarity and acuity. He was less thrilled with Abe's crotchety attitude.

"What?" Andre had the green-lensed glasses and the knife on his lap. He sat on the chair opposite his grandfather.

Coming Up Short 9

"Go to the hallway. Be careful that no one notices you. When the coast is clear, slip those glasses on. Take a look around at the people in the hall. See what you notice." Abe motioned him to go. "Go look around, but don't let them see the glasses."

Andre didn't move. He didn't need to go anywhere. "If you're talking about what these glasses turn people into, I've seen it. A couple of giant thugs came after me at the cabin."

Abe's eyes widened. "All the way out there?"

"Yes."

"Those glasses don't turn anyone into anything. They only reveal them for who they are. They help you see the monsters from everyone else. Without those glasses, those bastards look like normal people."

"So those guys were…they really were what I saw with the glasses on?"

"Yes." Abe pointed at the knife on Andre's lap. "That blade is the only way to kill them, but if they know you have it, they'll kill you to get it, and the glasses."

"How is this possible?" Andre wondered aloud.

"There's no time for that; those need to be hidden."

Coming Up Short 9

"What does monstrum interfectorem mean?" Andre began to hold up the knife to show Abe the inscription, but quickly dropped his hand to the far side of the chair. With his other hand, he stashed the glasses next to his leg. Beyond his grandfather, the room door opened, and a tall male nurse entered. Andre considered that his grandpa had a point regarding the staff at the facility. They were constantly in his room for one reason or another.

"Good afternoon." The nurse stopped next to his grandpa's desk, where a chart hung on the wall. "Is everything alright?" His eyes were on Andre.

"Yes, they are. Thank you for asking. Grandpa is having a good day, it seems."

Abe twisted in his chair and said to the nurse. "It was good until you got here."

The man smiled. "Same old Abe. Good to see you're feeling like yourself." He turned away to make a note on the chart hanging from a hook on the wall.

While the man had his back to them, Abe glanced at Andre. He touched his pointer fingers to the tips of his thumbs and held his hands up to his eyes. The circles he made were an indication that he wanted Andre to put on the glasses. Abe nodded over his shoulder at the nurse.

Look through the lenses at him.

Coming Up Short 9

Andre understood what the old man wanted and glanced at the nurse. The guy was still involved in his note-taking.

Though he wanted to sit perfectly still and keep the glasses out of sight, the temptation was too much. His grandfather was suspicious that the creatures were operating in the nursing home. Andre wanted him to be wrong. The idea the old man was surrounded by monsters was a horrible one. With a last glance at the back of the nurse, he pulled the glasses free from their hiding place and slipped them on his face.

His stomach cramped at first sight of what the nurse had become. Andre watched black wavering mists stream toward the ceiling from the back of the large man. They drifted up like slow-moving flames locked in a time warp. Above the neck of the nursing scrubs the creature wore, the same cracked skin with burning bright embers underneath was present. On the back of the nurse's head, flames simmered, and the air rippled around him.

Andre wanted to leap from his chair with a scream and sprint as far from the nursing home as possible. Nothing he had ever experienced had prepared him for a world with clandestine monsters as a part of it. So many questions swirled through his head that he felt dizziness overtaking him. While he wanted to flee, his body wasn't in lock-step with his desires. He felt paralysis creep through his body.

Coming Up Short 9

He felt Abe's gaze on him, but he couldn't bring himself to peel his eyes off the monster. It was as if he had consumed a hallucinogenic and couldn't get his mind to recall how it should operate.

The creature in Abe's room spun around to stare at him. The man, monster, or whatever he was had known something was off the moment he'd entered the room.

The same strange condition afflicted the front of the beast as had the back of it. Like the two goons at the cabin, blazing orange light burned under his skin. Jagged fissures on his cheeks allowed the light to seep through. His eyes set deep into his skull. They blazed an angry stoplight red at Andre.

"You have them!" the creature squealed.

He's talking about the glasses, dipshit! You should have taken them off!

Andre found confusion and panic to be his only friends. Abe sat unmoving in his chair, his mouth open and gaping like the Grand Canyon.

Andre attempted to hurl himself out of his seat. He pushed with one hand against an armrest, but flopped back into the seat when his shoes slipped on the tile floor.

Coming Up Short 9

It was the opening the creature needed. It leaped across the distance between them and landed on Andre, knocking him and the chair over backward. They landed with a thud on the floor; Andre staring up into the torch the monster's face had become. The creature returned his gaze. They locked eyes, and Andre thought he might go mad with the blazing red embers penetrating his mind. The heat pulsating from its head would undoubtedly burn his skin if he couldn't get the creature off his chest. Rancid breath pushed into his open mouth and up his nose. The urge to puke rolled up his throat, and he swallowed it down.

"Give them to me!" the monster demanded, as it snaked a hand around his throat. "Take them off and set them to the side!"

"Get…off…me…" Andre cried as he wriggled under the massive weight of the monster.

"Dammit! Use the knife, Al, it's in your hand!" Abe's voice came to him from above and a few feet away. The old man wasn't strong enough to help him, but he was right. Andre needed to take action, or he would soon die.

Andre squeezed his left hand tight around the knife handle. It vibrated in his grasp.

It feels alive…it wants to kill…

Coming Up Short 9

Such sentiment was irrational and stupid, but it was also real. The knife bucked in his hand, itching to lash out and stab the creature in the side.

"Dammit, Al! He's going to throttle the life out of you!" Abe screamed.

No truer words had ever been spoken. Already, Andre watched his field of vision narrow. When people talked about having near-death experiences, and they talked about tunnel vision, they weren't kidding. His eyesight was fading fast. So was the strength in his limbs. A strange tingling sensation had overtaken his hand. He knew he needed to stab the creature and yet it was hard to keep his thoughts clear.

"Oh, for fuck's sake!" He heard Abe curse.

The creature on his chest wobbled for a moment, which seemed to surprise it. Something had hit it. The sudden movement had surprised it as much as it had Andre.

What happened?

As the monster began to spin its burning head around, the knife was plucked from Andre's vibrating hand. He considered that his last chance to live had just gone away from him and he quickly realized he didn't care. If he had the strength, or air to speak, he would announce his intentions to make like a tree and leaf. Abandoning the battle and his physical body was in his best interest. Dying slowly was no fun at all. The world was leaving him, or he was leaving it. It was time to go, and he was A-okay with it. The coming darkness was his respite from the violence of the moment.

On his way to an escape into a black void of nothingness, the last of his eyesight brought him a strange scene. The monster choking the life out of him jerked upright. Its mouth opened, and a bright, burning red glow burst forth. It shook and tilted off him and finally fell to the floor, where it twitched as though an electric current ripped through it. As it dropped away, its hands fell away from Andre's throat.

With the weight gone from his chest, and the stranglehold gone from his throat, air rushed into his burning lungs, and he coughed. He coughed again and again while sitting upright. "Damn, that hurts!" He squawked and pulled in more air.

"Get up right now!" Abe demanded.

"Trying to breathe!" Andre choked out as he settled into a couple of last gagging gasps.

"If you don't move your ass, we're both dead meat on a stick!" Abe bent over and grabbed his toppled chair. "Here, help me get this upright!"

Andre pushed the chair back onto its feet.

Coming Up Short 9

"Now, pull those glasses off your face and put them in your pocket with the knife!" The old man handed him the knife. "Get them out of sight!"

It's clean. He stabbed the creature, but it's clean...

Andre did as he was instructed. He stood, stuffed his pockets with the glasses and knife, and plopped into the chair. He imagined his face was beet red as he regained his oxygen.

"They'll come looking for him." Abe collapsed in his chair. "Pretend like we're laughing and having a grand old time!" Abe pointed at him. The old man's face was tight with stress. "Laugh! It'll explain why you look like a tomato, son."

He knows who I am finally.

Andre felt the swelling in his throat. "Jesus, I can't laugh. I almost died!"

"If you don't laugh, you're going to die for damned sure!" Abe started chuckling, though his face still frowned.

"Where'd that guy go?" Andre glanced around the room.

Coming Up Short 9

Abe laughed as though Andre was on stage at improv night. "They just disappear into a ball of light! Poof!"

"Gone?"

Abe slapped a palm down on his thigh. "Completely! Now laugh, dammit!"

Andre forced a fake chuckle out of his sore throat. "That's hilarious, Grandpa!"

As he faked humor and pleasure, the door opened. Andre glanced up to see another hulking male nurse lean into the room. The man's eyes passed between them before saying, "You two seem to be having a good time."

Abe giggled again, "Boy, aren't we! This grandson of mine sure has a collection of great jokes." He glanced at Andre. "That last one was sure a doozy!"

The nurse, with short cropped blonde hair, reminded Andre of one of the old wrestlers, Hulk Hogan. His face seemed to growl the same as the Hulk had. His gaze fell on Andre. "Oh yeah? I like a good joke as much as the next guy. Lay it on me." His stare stayed locked on Andre.

He doesn't believe us. He's one of them.

Coming Up Short 9

"The joke, yeah of course, well, I mean…it's a little, uh, crass. I probably shouldn't repeat it." He tried opting out of any comedy routines, though the look on the nurse's face said the man wasn't buying.

"That's the best kind of joke. Try me." The man, or monster, wasn't going anywhere until he heard himself a gut buster.

"Uh, well…" Andre racked his mind for a joke. One of his friends, Peter, always had something funny to offer, if he could only remember the last time he'd been around Peter. "So, it goes like, uh…" He faked another chuckle to stall for time.

"You just told it and already you've forgotten?" Abe rolled his eyes and said to the nurse. "And I'm the one in the nursing home, huh?" Abe turned in his chair. "Okay, I'll tell him for you, mister shyness. Geez, kids these days, am I right?" The old man pivoted to face the nurse. "Alright, you're going to love this." He cleared his throat and asked, "Do you know how Burger King got Dairy Queen pregnant?"

The nurse, whose name badge was too far away for Andre to read, gazed at Abe. "No."

Abe grinned. "He forgot to wrap his whopper." The old man snickered, but kept an appraising eye on the large man.

Coming Up Short 9

The nurse stared at Abe before his eyes flicked back to Andre. His expression switched from a stern look of distrust to a neat little smile and a quivering chin. He did his best to force away a hidden snicker but finally succumbed to it. He laughed out loud and slapped a giant palm against the door frame. "Wrap his whopper." He laughed again, spittle dribbling from his gaping mouth. His laughter overcame him, and he made no attempt to stop it. "It shouldn't be as funny as it is, and yet…" He laughed again and leaned over. "Damn, that's one of the funniest things I've ever heard." He repeated the words of the joke while trying to pull in a chest full of air. "Burger King forgot to wrap his danged whopper! Hilarious!"

Abe glanced at Andre and shrugged. It was probably the only joke the old man could pull out of his head and it worked. Andre stared at his grandfather; his sore neck forgotten. The old man was a certified badass. He could not only slay the monsters, but he could also crack them up.

Who are you, Abe Lujan?

The nurse straightened and wiped tears from his eyes. "Geez, I needed that." He sighed. "I'll be laughing about it all day now." He turned to leave the room. "Oh! Have you guys seen Jose? He was supposed to stop by here on his way to spell me at the front desk."

Andre pretended to be testing his memory. "Well, I sure haven't seen him since I've been here."

Coming Up Short 9

"Huh." The nurse shrugged. "Well, he'll turn up."

No, he won't. Not ever again.

"Well," the nurse waved as he exited the room. "Have yourselves a whopper of a day!"

His laughter lingered as the door closed.

"I need to get you out of here, grandpa," Andre said. He stood from the chair and examined the tile floor. Not a single mark or blemish indicated the death of Jose, the monster. "Shit! What am I going to do?"

"Monster killer." Abe informed him from his chair "Monstrum interfectorem, it means monster killer. That's what the knife handle inscription says." He leaned forward in his chair. "I'm in no danger right now, unless they figure out that I know where the glasses and knife are. You need to go hide them, and don't tell a soul, including me, where they are because if they find them, we won't be able to defend ourselves."

Andre stared at the closed room door. "What good are the glasses and knife if we can't use them?"

Abe responded. "I'm not saying not to use them, but you can't keep them on you, or out in the open. They want nothing more than to find and destroy them. There were only a handful of them made and of those, only a few remain."

Coming Up Short 9

"So, what? You want me to kill monsters in the future?" Andre waited for a moment. When he didn't get a response, he glanced at his grandpa. The old man's glazed-over expression worried him. "Grandpa?"

Abe's tired eyes flicked to him. "Al, I'm getting tired and probably need a nap." He yawned.

"But what about hiding the glasses and knife?"

"The church. Remember the church?" Abe was gone again, completely off the reservation.

The old man waved a hand. "I can't recall what I was thinking about. It's the damn meds they've got me on." He stretched and tilted his reclining chair back. "I don't want to be rude, Al, but I'm going to get some shuteye. Thanks for visiting me. Tell your wife I said hello. Maybe we can visit some more when we go into town."

Andre wanted to cry. Not since Abe's initial diagnosis had he felt such despair. "Yeah, you should rest up. I'll go check out the church if I can figure out which one it is, and you get some sleep."

Already, Abe's eyes had closed, and his breathing was slowing. "That place…" He shuddered in his sleep.

★★★

Coming Up Short 9

"Where's Grandpa's old church?" Andre waited through his mother's silence.

"What's this all about?" She asked. The irritation in her voice angered him, but he hid the sentiment the best he could.

"Where did grandpa go to church?" He wouldn't play her game. She was nosey, and she had no right to be. She had nothing to do with him otherwise, so why should he accommodate her interrogation?

"Your grandfather never went to church. He's a believer, but he wasn't into church activities." Her voice was cool. Not answering her question pissed her off.

"Then why is he talking about a church?" Andre asked, making it clear he didn't believe her.

The irritation in Charlotte's voice came through in her answer. No longer was she willing to try to be civil. "Why the hell are you asking all these questions lately? He's an old man with dementia who can't even recall who he is most of the time."

"He has Huntington's mother." The mental barrier preventing him from ripping into her was deteriorating, and she knew it.

God, it's like she wants me to scream at her.

Coming Up Short 9

"Same thing. Maybe you need to accept that your grandpa is fading, and the fact is that he won't be with us much longer." She sighed. "I'm sorry to have to say that, but it's true."

His anger rose until he felt it spilling over. The ability to withhold it was gone. "Then, since you believe that to be true, you should visit him sometime. He did a lot for you, Mother. Have you forgotten that? Should we have you screened for Huntington's as well? Maybe it runs in the family."

The silence between them drew out long enough that he contemplated hanging up on her.

"Your grandfather got married in the old Lutheran church downtown on Fourth Street. That's what he was talking about." She slowed her voice, doing her best to sound like she was above his petty bickering. "Now, I have a life to live. If there's nothing else for your Highness, I need to go."

Before Andre could tell his mother that she was a lousy drunken idiot who had done nothing but embarrass him and his family, she ended the call.

★★★

Andre had only been checking out the grounds of the old church when the front door of the building opened, and a pastor exited. The man, as old as his grandfather, offered a friendly smile and crossed the grounds to greet him.

"Hello, I saw you out here from my office window and thought I should see if I could help you with anything."

The religious man was being polite. What he really wanted was to determine why Andre was trespassing. "So, you don't like strangers wandering around your church unannounced, huh?" Andre laughed. He needed to be friendly. Abe hadn't given him much to work with when it came to the church. For all he knew, he was at the wrong church entirely.

"Something like that, although it sounds rather inhospitable, and for that, I'm sorry. Sometimes, in this part of town, we get people who come around, and they…" The old man paused, scratched the thinning white hair on his head, and said, "Let's just say they don't have the best of intentions sometimes."

Andre introduced himself. "I apologize for interrupting your day. My name is Andre Lujan and I'm…"

"Abe Lujan? Is it possible you're related to him?" The old pastor's face fell slack. His eyes explored Andre from head to toe. "You'll have to pardon me, but you look like him. Is Abe your grandfather?"

Andre nodded his head. "He sure is."

Coming Up Short 9

"Wow. All these years later. Amazing."

"Why is it amazing? Have you seen my grandfather in the past few years?" Andre asked.

"No, I sure haven't, but he made a memorable impression on me." The old pastor extended his hand. "I'm Pastor Luke. I married your grandfather and his wife. I was relatively young and inexperienced back then, but Abe trusted me and, from what I understand, they had a wonderful marriage for many years."

After shaking his hand, Andre verbalized the thought running through his mind. "Maybe that's why my grandpa wanted me to come here." Andre thought about his grandfather. He'd been trying to tell Andre something about the church but had faded too fast.

"He wanted you to come here?" The pastor seemed surprised.

"Yes, at least I think so." He sighed. The glasses and knife were in his pocket. He could make things very easy by bringing them out, but intuition told him to leave them right where they were. "Did my grandfather ever tell you anything weird?"

"Yeah." The old man nodded and glanced around the front of the church building. "He sure did, and I've never forgotten it. So, I'll come out with it. If you're talking about those old glasses and knife, we better take this conversation inside."

Coming Up Short 9

★★★

Andre sat on the other side of the pastor's desk in his office at the back of the old church. Sitting behind the old cherry wood desk, the pastor looked as though he was running an extensive financial institution rather than a church in a small town. The desk was impressive and indicated wealth one didn't typically find in a church. Even the custom-built cherry shelves behind his desk spoke to a man of power, not religion.

Pastor Luke stared back at Andre while contemplating where to begin. Andre hoped the man had some helpful information. Anything would be helpful.

Pastor Luke sat still for a long amount of time and finally, with a sad sigh, spoke. "Do you have the glasses and knife?"

"No." He didn't waver or hesitate with his answer. It was an outright lie and flew out of his mouth far too easily, but he said it with a straight face. If his grandpa was right, they couldn't afford for anyone else to know where the antiquities were, although he could feel the lump of both in his pocket. They pressed against his right thigh. "My grandpa told me to hide them and never tell anyone where they were, so I did him one better. I asked someone to hide them for me. That way, I don't even know where they are." He was pleased with his bullshit answer, although God probably frowned on lying to a pastor. "This keeps anyone who knows about the glasses and knife safe, including you, since we're discussing this now."

"I'm sure your grandpa had good intentions in telling you that, but it may not be for the best." Pastor Luke held up a hand, silencing Andre's response. "Allow me to explain."

"Ok."

"Andre, have you looked through those glasses?"

This part he wouldn't lie about. He wasn't a good enough poker player to pull it off. "Yes, and I've seen the monsters. It's no joke. I don't know who or what they are, but they exist. They're real."

"Absolutely." Pastor Luke agreed with him. "Do you know the history of who they are?"

"No."

At least that's the truth. Suddenly. I've become a rather accomplished liar and telling the truth feels weird.

Pastor Luke shifted in his chair so that he could lean on his desk. He made a steeple of his hands, and it reminded Andre that he was in a church. "The beings you've seen are the ancestors of the witch of Endor. Do you know the biblical story about this witch?"

Coming Up Short 9

Andre allowed his gaze to roam over the volumes of old literature on the shelves behind the Pastor's desk. Surely the man possessed great knowledge on many subjects. "No, I've never heard of that before."

"In First Samuel, the Good Book discusses King Saul's desire to consult with a witch so that he could summon the spirit of the prophet Samuel. He wanted advice on how to defeat the Philistines. Previously, Saul had banned necromancy and magic, so he had to disguise himself to visit the witch in the night. He did this to hide his identity. Anyway, the witch brought forth the spirit of Samuel, but the spirit didn't give Saul what he wanted."

"What did the spirit give him?" Andre found the story fascinating and wondered why he'd never heard it before.

The pastor leaned back in his seat. "It predicted Saul's doom and gave him no advice regarding the Philistines. Saul broke his own rules only to learn of his coming death. The interaction also served to embolden the witch, who, in time, mated with a human male, and that is the beginning point for the race of people you've seen through the green glasses."

"Interesting." The biblical history only made him feel more creeped out by the creatures.

The pastor agreed. "Yes, and that's what makes the glasses and knife so important. Those beings are evil,

Coming Up Short 9

Andre. The church desperately wants them to fight against this evil."

"They tried to kill me. A couple of times." Andre informed him.

"Of that, young man, I have no doubt. They don't like people, but know they must hide their true identities to survive. At one time in our history, there were many tools like those glasses and the knife. Now, not so much, and because of that, there are now more monsters than we can account for, which is a scary thing."

"So, where did the glasses and knife come from?" he asked.

Pastor Luke shrugged. "No one really knows, other than somewhere in Europe. They're European-made and were designed to kill the ancestors of the witch. I don't know much more about them."

"So, what do you think I should do?" Andre admitted. "Do you want me to give you the glasses?"

"I would like you to give them to the church, Andre, yes." He stared at Andre over the wooden desk.

"I could never do that without talking to my grandpa."

Coming Up Short 9

The pastor said, "Let's go see him now, together."

Andre felt the old man was well-intentioned, and maybe even right, but he would never disobey his grandpa's directions. Maybe the church was the right entity to battle the evil creatures, but the decision to hand over the glasses and knife wasn't his. "No, he's resting, but I'll chat with him." Andre stood. "Thank you, Pastor. I appreciate your time."

The old man jumped to his feet and hurried around his desk as Andre crossed the room to the exit. "Wait! You're in over your head on this. At least allow me to help you. I've known your grandfather for many years. I'm sure he'll be on board with my plan once he knows it."

"I'll keep it between me and him, but if he wants to speak with you about it, I'll let you know. Thanks again." Andre turned away.

As he moved, the pastor grabbed his arm. "Andre! Maybe you should stay here until we know you're alright. By now, I'm sure the creatures know about you and are seeking you out."

Andre pulled his arm away. The old man released him without clinging, for which he was grateful. "I'll be fine, but thank you for offering."

Coming Up Short 9

"Okay, but please come back soon. We need to keep the world safe."

Andre left the pastor standing on the threshold of his office and walked out of the church.

★★★

"What are we doing, Al?" Abe looked confused as Andre pushed him in a wheelchair down the main hall of the nursing home.

"We're getting you out of here."

"For a walk?"

Andre noticed the slight tremble in his grandpa's arms. The sight made him feel sick to his stomach. The old man had always been a symbol of strength. Abe Lujan had always seemed indestructible. It was hard to see him looking like a frail older man. "Yeah, a walk and a drive."

"Why are you taking me, Al?"

"Why not?" Andre struggled to answer his questions. Watching every door for one of the nurses or orderlies that seemed to be everywhere in the facility was distracting work. "If you remember the glasses and the blade, that's why."

Coming Up Short 9

"What glasses? Did you lose your glasses?" Abe asked.

Andre ignored Abe as he approached the front desk of the nursing home. Either God had smiled on him, he was lucky, or he should be far more paranoid than he was. The desk was empty.

Don't waste time.

He pushed Abe toward the exit and prayed he would make it to his car without being seen or noticed. Through exiting the building and crossing the parking lot, Abe asked a million questions about his eyewear and why they were leaving the farm.

Andre promised to answer his questions once they were on the road. He'd spent the entire night rethinking his conversation with Pastor Luke and had determined his grandfather should talk to the man. After all, he'd sent him to the church for a reason. The only way to make a visit possible, without exposing where Abe lived, though, was to bring him to Luke. If the conversation went well, they could hand over the glasses and knife. If not, they'd retreat, and he'd need a new plan. It was the only way to protect his grandpa and get the information he needed.

As Abe crawled into the car, he asked, "Where are we going, Al?"

"To church, Grandpa."

Coming Up Short 9

"Well, dammit. I never did like going to hear what a sinning piece of shit I am." The old man grumbled, "Truth hurts, I guess."

★★★

"Abe Lujan! Welcome!" Pastor Luke vigorously shook Abe's hand. "It's so good to see you after so many years!" To Andre, he added, "Thank you so much for bringing him here. I want you two safe, and I want us to end the expansion of evil here in our little town. So, thank you for coming."

Abe asked him, "Do we know each other? I'm afraid my memory isn't quite what it used to be."

Luke guided them into the church lobby and said, "Why don't we visit in my office? Do you recall the way?" he asked Andre.

"Sure, I can get us there."

"Wonderful. I have something to finish up, which will only take a minute, and I'll be right with you."

Before, he didn't want me out of his sight. Now he sends me to wander through his church.

Pastor Luke excused himself and entered a dark hall on the side of the foyer.

Coming Up Short 9

He sure moves with some pep at his age.

Andre guided his grandpa down through the entrance, into the naïve, and past the sanctuary to the small office tucked at the back of the building. The door was open, and Andre guided Abe inside, allowing the door to fall closed behind them. "This is the church where…"

"Where I was married." Abe stared at the giant bookshelves behind the desk.

"Exactly! You remember?" Andre asked. His voice hitched in his chest. It was the moments Abe was himself that he craved.

"Dre?" Abe looked at him. "What the hell are we doing here?"

"Well, Pastor Luke, he knows all about the…"

"Damn right, he does. Who told you about this place?" Abe was incensed. He also seemed fearful.

Andre stood next to him, unable to hide his confusion. "You did."

"Me?"

"Well, you and mom. She gave me the address." Andre admitted.

Coming Up Short 9

Abe spun in a circle, seeking a way to escape. "Shit! We have to get out of here!" He hurried to the office door and tossed it open. "Let's go!"

"But why? What's the problem?" Andre asked as he chased after Abe. "Slow down and tell me what's going on." He tried to keep his voice down, though he wasn't sure why.

Abe rounded the sanctuary and entered the center of the naïve. "If I mentioned this place, it was to keep you away from here."

Andre caught up to him halfway toward the church lobby. "I don't understand."

The double doors at the head of the naïve opened and a slender figure entered. She moved in her usual enticing manner, her hips rolling from side to side as she stepped.

Andre skidded to a stop next to his grandfather. The sight of the woman who had entered the room confused him. She was the most beautiful woman he'd ever seen, but completely out of place in the church. Either she was having one over on him, or her presence in the church was one of the biggest coincidences of all time. "What are you doing here, Arden?"

"Who's she?" Abe asked.

Coming Up Short 9

"My roommate," Andre replied. "And I didn't know she went to church here. I guess it's a small world."

Abe's mouth hung open; he gaped at her. "Good God, how'd you ever get any sleep?"

Arden grinned as she sauntered toward them, one of her hands trailing along on the wood edge of the pews. Her fingers were like the rest of her, long, pretty, and lean. With her voice low and smooth, she said, "Oh, you know better than that, Dre. Think about it."

"Why are you here?" Andre heard himself ask her.

"The good pastor called me, well, us, as far as that goes, I guess." She snickered.

Behind her, the church doors swung open again. Another woman entered.

"Mom?"

"Jesus, Mary, and Joseph. Well, this explains a lot," Abe said as he stared at his daughter. "They got to you too, huh?"

Charlotte stepped next to Arden and stopped walking. She offered a little wave of her fingers to Andre. "Hi, son."

Coming Up Short 9

"You're not his mother. You're what happens when one of those things kills a person. They steal their identity." Abe said. His feet were planted on the carpet square with his shoulders. Andre knew the old man was ready for a fight.

"You're not my mom?" Andre asked, realizing there was more to the personality changes in her than he had previously imagined. Her being an absolute idiot most of the time made sense if she was one of the creatures.

Charlotte and Arden stepped forward once and stopped. "Oh, Dre, it's so much less painful than you think." Charlotte offered a fake grin as she spoke. There wasn't an ounce of sincerity in it.

"Andre, put the glasses on. See for yourself," Abe told him.

He pulled the glasses from his pocket, already sure of what he'd see, but needing to see it, anyway. With the lenses on his nose, he stared ahead at the two women. Each had fire in her eyes, wafting black tendrils of gray flames flickering high above them, and orange cracks in their skin. The glow emanated from the fire burning in their skulls.

Andre removed the glasses from his face and returned them to his pocket. "Thanks for sending me here, ma."

Coming Up Short 9

She laughed. "My poor boy."

"Come on, Grandpa, we're going out the back, and these two are going to leave us the hell alone." He sneered at his mother and Arden.

Before he could turn away, a vise-like pair of arms wrapped around him from behind. "Not so fast, boy," Pastor Luke spoke into his ear. "We can't have you out there running around knowing about us, now, can we?"

"You leave me and grandpa alone!" Though Andre struggled against the old pastor, he couldn't pry himself free. The old monster was much stronger than he appeared.

"That's right, Andre." Another man stepped around him from behind. The white lab coat gave him away before Andre could see his face.

"Dr. Williams?"

"That's right." The doctor said with a chuckle.

Andre watched his grandfather approach the doctor from behind. He wanted to warn him away. Abe was only going to jeopardize his health. "Wait! We can talk about this. If you'd just…"

Dr. Williams plunged a hypodermic needle filled with an amber fluid into his arm. "There you go. Now relax, Andre. It's all going to be fine." The doctor spoke in a soothing voice.

Before Andre could fall to the carpeted, naïve floor, his body had gone limp, and a warm sensation worked its way across his chest. The world seemed to spin around him. In the movement, he saw his grandpa caught between his mother and Arden. The old man was in trouble, and it was all Andre's fault. His failing mind knew he should never have brought the old man to the church.

These thoughts and others worked through his head, but he could no longer focus on them.

The lights in the church seemed to turn off. Maybe God had changed his mind about their being light in the world.

★★★

"Dre, can you hear me?" The voice coming to him through layers of fog and haze was familiar. It was a pretty voice belonging to someone attractive and very feminine. That much he remembered. Everything else he knew about the person was gone. It had wandered off into the wilderness and into a new life, and that life was one that no longer included him.

He pried his tired eyes open and stared at a gorgeous brunette who stared back at him. She smiled at him, but it wasn't a friendly kind of grin. It was more how he imagined a wolf would grin at a rabbit before pouncing.

Because he was male, even her obviously poor intentions weren't enough to keep him from admiring her good looks. "Who are you?" His mouth was dry, and his voice sounded like dried up, heated over shit.

"Awe." Her lower lip protruded, and she winked at him. "You don't remember me?" The giggle she made told him she wasn't really all that surprised by his vacant mind.

"We've met before, right?" he asked, partially afraid of the answer.

"So, you don't know who I am at all?" She lingered next to his bed, the fingers of her right hand trailing up his hand and wrist.

"No."

She allowed her hand to drop away from his arm. "Oh, I'm so sad. We used to be roommates, that was, until you had your accident."

"Accident?" His heartbeat picked up its pace.

"Yes, unfortunately, you fell and hit your head very hard, and now you have…uh, what did they call it?" Her eyes tilted up and she searched the ceiling for the right word.

Coming Up Short 9

As she stared into her memory, a door opened behind her and a man in a white lab coat entered the room. "Hello, Andre. How do you feel?"

"Who are you?"

The man in the coat replied, "I'm Dr. Williams. You've suffered some memory loss. You damaged your hippocampus in an accident, but don't you worry. We're doing everything we can to help you."

"I don't remember hitting my head." He tried to sit up and realized his wrists were shackled to the bed frame.

"They're for your own protection." The doctor tilted his head toward the metal bands.

"When can I get out of here?" Andre returned his gaze to the pretty brunette. "Who did you say you are again?"

The doctor placed a hand against his cheek. "This is going to take some time. Eventually, we'll get you there." The doctor removed his hand. "By the way, has your grandfather been here? Would you remember if he came by?"

"I don't remember a grandpa." Andre blinked his eyes. "Who are you guys again? I feel a little fuzzy."

Coming Up Short 9

The doctor moved away from his bed. "I'll check on you later. We'll see if you can recall anything more at that time."

He watched the two people move toward the door the doctor had entered through. The woman, who walked behind the doctor, had a nice shape to her. She was pretty. He could tell, even from behind. Though she had just been standing next to him, already her face was fading from his mind.

The man in his room with the woman had said he'd had an accident of some kind, but he couldn't recall what he'd injured. It was hard to remember much of anything.

Andre closed his eyes. Maybe someday he would remember.

★★★

"Hey, kid. Remember me?"

The old man standing next to his bed was removing the painful metal things from around his wrists. The man glanced up. As he moved, little wisps of gray hair waved. Though he didn't know the man, he had kind eyes, kind but feisty. He bet the old guy could still hold his own in many ways.

"Who are you?"

Coming Up Short 9

"I'm your grandpa." The man unbound his right wrist and moved around the bed. "We don't have much time. We're going to get you up and out of here."

Andre liked the idea of having a grandpa, although he didn't remember the old guy at all. "I had an accident."

"Bullshit, you did!" the man cursed. "They did this to you with medication like they did to me, the damned liars."

After a moment, Andre's other hand was free from its binds. He raised his arms and flexed his hands. "Thank you. That feels so much better."

The old man hurried back around the bed. He held up a pair of old glasses with green lenses and a long knife. "Do you remember these?"

A flash of standing in a church entered his mind. The old man had been with him. So had the glasses. He had been wearing them. "They stole them from me. I don't know how I know that, though. Is it true?"

"Sure as hell it is, but I got them back." The old man handed him a pair of jeans. "We're going to get you up and get you into these. Then we're going to leave before they realize I'm here."

"Okay." Andre pushed the covers away from his legs. "Then what will we do?"

Coming Up Short 9

The old man stared at him. The expression on his face was one of hatred and a willingness to fight to the bitter end. "We're going to kill ourselves a lot of creatures."

QUELLER

It was one of those lazy Saturday afternoons where nothing was important, and the day presented so many opportunities to relax and forget about work, chores, and bills that she felt like she could get lost in happiness forever. It was only her and Mark, her husband, just as she preferred it. They held hands as they progressed down the small downtown shopping area.

The aged buildings, street parking spaces, and the Christmas lights strung along the winter barren trees all lent to the atmosphere and her good mood. "Isn't this nice?" She asked him.

"For sure. They always do such a nice job down here around the holidays. I'm grateful to live in a small town. In the city, we'd be up to our necks in pick pockets and dealers out on a downtown sidewalk like this."

She smiled and squeezed his hand. "Yes, I'm so grateful to be done with all that. Moving here was the right thing to do, for both of us, and for our collective sanity, but I was thinking more about today. It's so nice to be together and have no Monday through Friday worries, isn't it?"

"It sure is." He kissed her forehead.

She loved it when he did it. It was an act of genuine love from the man she couldn't live without. He was her heart and soul and always had been.

Coming Up Short 9

They side-stepped a little boy who had wandered away from his mother while eating his ice cream cone. While his mother yelled at him for leaving her side, Mark said to his wife, "Yeah, if every day could be Saturday, I'd be perfectly content. At least we both work from home these days. No commute."

Maggie grinned and pointed to an upcoming jewelry store. "Let's go look, okay?"

"Sure, then we'll find some lunch." He said.

She stopped on the sidewalk and turned to face him. "Love you."

"Love you, too."

She reached up to kiss him. On her way, she said, "Just remember how much you love me while we're in the jewelry store. You never know, I might find something I like."

Mark laughed while kissing her. "Very sneaky, Mrs. Adams."

She pivoted and pulled him forward. "You know I'm a sucker for jewelry. I might even give you some Christmas hints in there. So, pay attention." She allowed her eyes to take in the scene around them on her way into the small shop. Winter had fully overtaken the fall. Christmas was a month away and the downtown shopping area was fully decorated for the occasion. Many people were out shopping in the unique little stores and the gray sky seemed pregnant with hope. It was a perfect representation of her mood.

Coming Up Short 9

The future seemed bright. She had no concrete reason for this, and she was alright with it that way.

The days ahead were bright, their future full of promise. They lived in the perfect place, and she was married to the perfect man.

Mark held the door open for her and she entered The Netherworld Jewelry Company.

★★★

Upon entering the jewelry store, Maggie noticed a few things. The place smelled of old leather combined with a pine-scented household cleaner. She also noticed an elderly gentleman behind the sales counter. He had a full head of wavy gray hair, sparkling blue eyes that said he was much younger in spirit than years, and a pair of round reading glasses perched on the tip of his nose.

Dressed in a dapper gray and black suit and tie, he grinned at them and welcomed them into his shop. "Please, do come in. Help yourselves to peruse everything. We have both new pieces and antique offerings."

Maggie brushed her long blonde hair behind her shoulders and wondered if the old man noticed the stark contradiction between her and Mark's hair color. Most people did when meeting them for the first time. Mark was her exact opposite with jet-black hair. Of course, he was also a foot taller than her, but that wasn't all that unusual. She thanked the older man as they moved to a case at the center of the store.

Coming Up Short 9

"You're certainly welcome." He glanced out the front windows of his shop. "It's such a wonderful day, isn't it?"

The man had a soft timbre in his voice that made her feel perfectly at home, even though it was her first visit to his store. She'd never had a grandfather, but he would have done nicely. His dress and mannerisms screamed sophistication.

"It sure is." Maggie agreed. She bent over to peer into the glass cabinet before her. Mark pressed against her to look over her shoulder.

She perused multiple rings with stones of all varieties inside the case. None of them had price tags on them, but each looked ultra-pricey. Several diamond rings lined up next to a row of ruby rings. Adjacent to these rows were rings with a variety of stones in them. Each sparkled and glistened under the bright lights of the display case.

As her eyes drifted lower, they fell on a ring with a simple, but broad band and a dark blue stone mounted on top. "Ooh, look at that one, hon. I love it."

"What kind of stone is that?" Mark leaned close to her. He also stared down into the case at the spectacular piece. "Is that a sapphire?"

"No, it's lapis lazuli. It's a rare, precious stone mined in Russia, Chile, and, of all places, Afghanistan." The elderly man moved behind the counter in their direction. He arrived in front of them and searched his pockets for a set of keys. "Now, that piece is older than the three of us put together."

Coming Up Short 9

"Really?" Mark asked. "Wow."

"Indeed, young man." The old man retrieved a set of keys from his pants pocket and unlocked the glass case. While sliding the door over, he said, "It was made in 1792, although its country of origin is under some scrutiny."

Maggie glanced up from the case. "What do you mean?"

"Well, most people believe it to be from Chile. Some believe Afghanistan. To me, it never mattered. It's a gorgeous piece, and I still have trouble believing I was able to get my hands on it." He reached into the case and removed the ring.

Once out of the case, Maggie could see its age in the band. The gold band looked as though it had been around long enough to see the world through multiple wars and several owners.

"Its precise history is a little cloudy, but here she is." The elderly man lowered his glasses away from his eyes but left them on his nose. "What size are you?"

"Six," Maggie answered.

"Are you sure, babe?" Mark asked.

Maggie blushed and replied in a short voice, "Yes, I'm sure, dear." Mark was referring to the slight weight gain she'd been complaining about, but she didn't want to have the conversation in front of the shop owner.

Coming Up Short 9

"Good news, then! This ring happens to be a modern-day six!" He reached the ring out to her and said, "Try it on if you like."

"Oh, wow." Maggie stuck out the ring finger on her right hand, allowing him to ease the ring over her knuckle and down her finger. As it slid over her skin, she thought she would swear to an entire team of bible carrying priests she could feel a strange energy coming from it.

The old man leaned away and pushed his glasses back up his nose. He stared down at her finger, smiled broadly, and shifted his gaze to them. "As I suspected, it looks perfect on you." He sighed, as though he had suddenly become the most satisfied man in the entire world. "It should be yours." He declared. "Sometimes, you can just see that a ring belongs to someone, and you and this ring are a made match!"

Mark cleared his throat, "Well, it's probably also very spendy, am I right?"

Maggie elbowed her husband, embarrassed that he was making them sound poor. "We can afford this if we want it." She rolled her eyes and spoke to the old shopkeeper. "My husband…"

"Mags, we don't even know…"

"Stop it!" The words came out of her mouth, loud and terse. So much so that she realized she was too loud and immediately apologized to the older man. "I'm sorry, but you know I don't like being called that. I guess I like the ring enough that I'm being a little feisty."

Coming Up Short 9

The old man extended his hand to her. "Your husband is right. I shouldn't be so presumptuous. He would also be right if he pointed out that I haven't even properly introduced myself." He shook his head at himself. "What an embarrassment I've become in my old age. If my son saw such behavior out of me, he would surely have something to say about it, that I can promise."

"Oh?" Maggie asked. "You have a son?"

"Sure do. He's planning on coming here one of these days."

"Where is he now?" She asked.

He took her hand in his. She at first recoiled from his freezing grip, but the sensation passed quickly. The old man answered, "He's in the south, but as I said, he'll be along any time now. Anyway, please forgive my rudeness. My name is Lived Southerly, and I am the owner and proprietor of The Netherworld Jewelry Company."

"That's an ominous name," Mark said.

Maggie glanced over her shoulder to glare at him. "Please forgive my husband and his suddenly very poor manners." She turned her attention back to Lived. "That's an interesting name."

"Yes, we have my father to thank for that one. It's spelled L.I.V.E.D. like someone who's lived a long time but pronounced like someone who's exceptionally angry, as in livid."

Coming Up Short 9

Maggie released his grip and held her right hand up in the light. "So, your father named you, but you don't like your name?" She contemplated his name. There was something to it, like a puzzle. It was probably because the old man was mysterious in an attractive sort of way. He had a depth about him that remained hidden under the surface.

He waved a hand. "I'm fine with the name. It's him I don't like so much. He was always so unfair. The name was meant to mark me, but I never let it bother me. In fact, I embraced my name just to provoke him." He sighed, his eyes vacant and in the past for a moment.

"I'm sorry to hear that." Mark offered.

He snapped out of his fog. "It's not to be upset about, and neither is he. Someday, I'll get my turn…"

"Your turn?" Maggie asked. She spoke to him but couldn't peel her eyes off her hand and the ring. It perfectly accentuated her fingers. In truth, she thought she might even have the hand of a model with the ring on. It was a beautiful piece.

Lived placed his hands in his pants pockets. "Let's turn our focus on this lovely ring. Ma'am, why don't you try to slide it up and down your finger? Let's see how well it fits."

Maggie tugged on the ring. Instead of sliding back up her finger, it pulled tight, taking her skin with it until it gathered at the lower edge of her knuckle. "Oh no, it didn't feel that tight when you put it on." She released the ring, and it snapped back into place. Again, the feeling that she should know more about the old man than she did came over her. It was like missing something or forgetting something that was right on the tip of her tongue. No matter how close it was, it was still a million miles away.

She turned away from the shop owner and held out her hand to Mark. "Will you help me get this wonderful ring off my hand?"

"Of course." Mark grasped her hand in his left and used the fingers on his right hand to grab the ring. While he tugged on the ring, he whispered to her, "I tried to warn you, you're not a six anymore."

He pulled on the ring until Maggie cried out in pain and ripped her hand away. "Why are you being so rough?" What Mark had done had hurt her, but the main reason she pulled back from him was that she wanted to keep the ring. She didn't want it off and the idea that she would ever be without it made her feel like falling to her knees and weeping openly.

Lived held out his hand. "Madam, if you don't mind."

Maggie stared into his eyes. The blue in them was as deep and ancient as the ocean. Dark wisdom existed there, and it was irresistible. She allowed him to take her hand in his. Once again, that feeling of ice on bare skin returned, and then it was gone as he released her hand.

Lived held up the ring. "There you go. No worries at all. It came right off."

"How'd you do that?" Mark asked, amazed.

Coming Up Short 9

"Oh, years of professional experience." Lived shrugged. "Do you want to know the ring's price?"

"Yes!" Maggie exclaimed. She hated the feeling of emptiness that overcame her. The ring and she had almost been one.

"Ten thousand." Lived replaced the ring in the case and locked the sliding door closed.

Mark snickered. "It's nice, but not that nice."

"Yes, it is…was," Maggie argued, though her voice was quiet and seemed far away.

"What's that, hon?" Mark wasn't questioning her opinion of the ring. Instead, he stared at her hand. He tapped her finger. "There's a word pressed into your skin where the ring was."

"What?" Maggie held her hand up again to the light. "Oh, my God. What is that?"

Lived leaned close to her hand. "Well, that's sure something. I've never seen that before."

She gazed down at her finger. A red ring of skin irritation encircled her finger, only interrupted by the bright red letters on the top of her finger. "Qhar." She read the letters. "I wonder what that means?"

Mark glanced at Lived, who was busy retrieving the ring from the case. "They must have stamped inside the ring for it to be pressed into her skin like that."

Coming Up Short 9

"Yes, I quite agree." The old man pulled the ring from the case and used a jeweler's glass from inside another of his pockets to inspect the ring's interior.

Maggie rubbed the skin on her finger where the word appeared. It seemed as though the antiquated piece of jewelry had tattooed her. The word wouldn't rub out, even though it had pressed into her skin.

"Sure enough. Wow." Lived pulled back from his inspection of the ring. "Those letters, Q, H, A, and R - are raised in the gold on the inside of the ring. It must have some sort of secret meaning. If I knew where the ring came from, I might be able to figure it out." He sighed and replaced the jewel in the glass cabinet.

Maggie smiled at the older man. She wasn't at all upset at the imprint on her finger. If anything, she felt honored that the ring had marked her.

"I'm sure in the next couple of hours that mark will be gone." Lived reassured her.

"I'm fine with it." She stared down at her finger. It was her hope the word, whatever it meant, wouldn't fade too quickly.

"Can I show you any other rings?" Lived asked.

"Oh, no. Thank you, though. We need to be moving along." Mark replied.

Lived smiled. Maggie noticed how his teeth were perfectly white and lined up in nice little rows. When she was his age, she wanted to be in as good shape. Lived was an impressive man. He spoke to her, a

Coming Up Short 9

wry grin still on his face. "Well, thank you for stopping in my shop. It isn't often such a handsome couple comes along. It was a pleasure meeting you both." As he stepped away, he nodded his head. "Have a good day, Maggie and Mark."

It wasn't until they were outside, and moving down the sidewalk, that Maggie realized what was on her mind since leaving the shop. "Did we tell him our names?"

"Huh?" Mark asked.

"Lived. You know, he knew our names. I couldn't remember if we introduced ourselves."

Mark tilted his head and squinted his eyes against the partial sun shining through the clouds. "I can't remember either. I guess I've been thinking about that print on your finger."

Maggie checked her finger. The word, Qhar, was still there, as bright as it had been in the shop. "Looks like it's going to take it a while to fade."

"Yeah, but what'd it mean?" He wondered.

"Google it." She suggested.

"Great idea." He pulled his phone out of his pocket and typed the word in a search bar. He scrolled through several of the listings that came up on the phone and then clicked the device off. "Weird."

"What does it mean?" She held her hand up to him. "Wait. Let me guess. Does it mean love?"

Mark glanced at her. "No, it doesn't."

"What does it mean, then?"

He reached for her hand and held it as they crossed the street at an intersection. "It's a word in a language called Dari. It's from the Middle East, Afghanistan in particular."

"So, that must be where the ring was originally made." She pondered. The knowledge made her want to own the ring more. Of course, she'd need to get it resized and rob a bank to pay for it. She glanced up at Mark. "Are you going to tell me the meaning of Qhar in Dari?"

"Anger." He shrugged his shoulders. "It means anger. Weird, right?"

★★★

"Dammit!" Maggie slammed her fist on the kitchen counter. "Why are you so persistent about this today?"

Mark set his book on the table and turned to glance at her. "Are you seriously angry about me wanting us to go to Maggiano's? I made us a reservation because I asked you yesterday and you said sure."

"Here you go again." Maggie tossed the cookie sheet with the dough balls into the sink. The little round pieces of dough all slid into the bottom of the sink and settled into murky water. "There, are you satisfied?" She turned to glare at Mark. He'd gotten on her nerves to the point she would rather do anything else than stay in the kitchen with him. It pissed her off to be told what she had committed to when she knew damn well she hadn't.

"Seriously?" Mark rolled his eyes. "You're acting like an overgrown child. You just wasted all that cookie dough because of a temper tantrum. Nice, Mags, real nice."

He shook his head, and she knew he did it to piss her off. How many times had she asked him not to be so condescending when they argued? It was incendiary, and it was precisely what he wanted it to be, but he'd deny it. "It was my dough to waste. I made it, you didn't!" She fired back.

Mark stood from the table. "Think about this for one second, alright? You're angry because your husband wants to take you to a nice dinner." He cranked up his exaggerated 'my name is Maggie and I'm a spoiled bitch' face. "Ooh, poor me, Mark is such as asshole. I can't stand him. He's so mean, taking me out to eat. I wish I had married someone who wouldn't do anything for me at all!"

She leaned against the counter, amazed at how insulting he could be sometimes. "I'm not mad because you wanted to take me to dinner. I'm upset because you never asked. You assume it's fine, but sometimes I might have something going on."

"And do you?" He glared at her.

Coming Up Short 9

She didn't, and he knew it, yet she couldn't get herself to say it. She returned his stare and folded her arms over her chest, unwilling to give him the satisfaction or the answer he wanted.

"Yeah, that's what I thought." He pushed the chair under the table. "I'm going to cancel the reservation. The last thing I would do now is take you out."

"Why don't you say it? I can see it written all over your face, so you may as well!" She said while hating herself for the quiver in her voice. It sounded weak and he would know she was on the verge of crying.

"Say what?" he glared at her, his nostrils flaring with his anger. "Why don't you tell me what I'm thinking? Apparently, you know me better than I know myself."

"That you think I'm a bitch!" She tossed the kitchen towel she had in her hands onto the counter.

"I don't think that, so quit putting words in my mouth." He pointed at her hand. "But I do think that word that's still visible on your finger has something to do with it."

She scoffed. "Don't be ridiculous."

"Look at your finger, Mags. That word, Qhar, or whatever, is still there, and it's been a week. You had that ring on your finger for three minutes and a week later, that imprint is still there."

Coming Up Short 9

She held up her hand. Though she wanted to scream at him for again not using her proper name, she ignored it. "It's fading. You can see that it's much lighter than it was before and it's dumb to blame the ring. It's not like it had some sort of supernatural power."

Mark threw his hands in the air and walked away. "Well, the word means anger and since you put that ring on, you sure have been."

★★★

"I'm sorry." She poked him in the leg with her toe under the covers.

Mark rolled over to face her in the dark. "What got into you?"

"I don't know. I guess I've been a little stressed lately, although I'm not sure why." Maggie's voice got quieter. "Will you forgive me for being a giant bitch today?"

"I already forgave you. I was just worried because that's way out of character behavior for you."

"I know." She sighed and placed an arm across his chest. "I'm an idiot as well as irrational."

Mark held her hand and kissed it. "Why do you say that?"

"Because Maggiano's sounds so good."

Coming Up Short 9

He pulled the covers over their interlocked hands to ward off a chill in the room. "We'll go another day. I'll surprise you."

"Promise?"

"Yup."

She kissed him goodnight on his cheek. "I'll be a good girl next time."

★★★

Going to the grocery store irritated her to no end. Rude people all doing their best to get in and out of the building as fast as they could, all trampling over one another without a care in the world. Maggie had no clue when the world had become such a violent and disturbing place, but she was sick of it.

Unfortunately, if you wanted your groceries delivered, that service came with unaffordable fees. Mark was too cheap to pay them, of course, so here she was, working her way through the aisles of the store with all the idiots in town. "Lucky me."

Ahead of her, a woman in a lengthy blue dress, long brown hair, and sneakers of all things stopped her cart in the middle of the aisle to walk to one side of the shelves. She stood, obstructing the lane, staring at one box of cereal after another.

A part of Maggie considered bumping the woman's cart out of her way with her cart, but another part of her insisted on the virtues of being civil. The woman was more than dumb and inconsiderate, but

Coming Up Short 9

patience was still a virtue, hopefully. She smiled, though it was fake, and said, "Excuse me, ma'am? Could you move your cart?"

The woman glanced at her, and without changing her expression at all, returned her gaze to a box of cereal, and said, "I'll be done in a minute."

Maggie felt the steam building inside her head. She imagined if she was a cartoon character, it would pour out of her ears while her face turned cherry red. She cleared her throat and said, "Yes, I'm sure you will, but I'm in a bit of a hurry and you're obstructing the lane. All you need to do is pull your cart over to the side with you instead of leaving it in the middle."

This time, though the woman spoke to her, she refused to look back at Maggie. "I said just a minute." Her tone was both stern and arrogant. How dare some stupid peasant bother her while she, the queen of the known universe, was busy shopping for cold, sugar-filled cereal.

The torch lit inside Maggie seemed to grow hotter. She flushed with hatred and venom laced her mouth. Maggie shrugged. If the woman wanted a confrontation, she was going to get one. "Okay, bitch, I tried to be nice!" Maggie rammed the woman's cart with her own and pushed hard. Though the cart was full and relatively heavy, it moved forward. She churned her legs until she ran down the aisle with both carts.

"Hey!" the lady screamed at her. "That's my cart!"

Coming Up Short 9

"Not anymore, you hag." The anger in her was born from the frustration she felt from being in the store for too long. She was aware of this, but once her temper had been engaged, she felt it take over her. It was impossible to resist. While her rage grew, she celebrated the feeling of power it gave her. The uptight bitch of a woman was going to learn to pull her goddamned cart over once and for all. In the future, she'd think twice about being so damned rude to others.

The slap of shoes on the tiled floor told Maggie the woman was in pursuit. Because of the weight of the two carts, she would easily catch up before Maggie could make it to the end of the aisle. The rational part of Maggie was long gone. Her pent-up rage was in the driver's seat and pushing the gas pedal to the floor. Rationality was a thing of the past.

Her anger told her what needed to be done. What she'd started in taking the cart from the woman was akin to poking the bear. She had irritated her and even pissed her off from the sounds the woman made as she huffed her way after Maggie, but no lessons would be imparted with that action alone. It was a first step, and a good one, but it wouldn't do any good without something more. No, if she wanted to teach the bitch a lesson…there was but one thing to do.

Maggie pushed forward, listening to the sounds the woman made as she gained on her. The woman was determined to catch up. The sounds of exertion and strain weren't hard to discern and for these little indicators of the woman's progress, Maggie was grateful. She needed the woman to get a little closer. She trusted her ears to tell her when the woman was within three or four feet. At that distance, she could act. The rude woman had no idea of the trap she'd fallen into as she pursued her groceries.

Footfalls grew louder, and the angered, harried woman gained on her. This was good. It was precisely what she wanted. Maggie released the cart handle and spun around while forming her right hand into a fist. She raised it up next to the side of her head while watching with glee as the woman realized something was very wrong. She'd expected Maggie to run away faster, not turn to fight.

The woman, with her hair flowing in the rushing air, tried to slide to a stop, but her momentum carried her too far forward. With her eyes wide, her nostrils flaring, and a parade of four-letter words flowing from her mouth, she slipped on the floor, tried her best to recover, and then completely tripped.

As she fell toward the floor, Maggie launched her fist at the woman. The swift blow connected solidly with her target in the middle of the woman's face. A satisfying crunch reverberated up her arm, and blood poured from the woman's nose before she could fall all the way down.

She wailed at Maggie. "You fuffing hit meh!"

Her voice sounded as though she had stuffed tissue up both of her nostrils. She had a plugged-up quality that Maggie found hilarious. "Ha!" she snickered as the woman tried to stop the bleeding.

The woman's hands found her nose as she knelt on her knees. Blood drained down through her fingers and onto her legs. In the palm of one of her hands, a little white stone lay with a couple of bloody trails attached to it. Once Maggie realized it was a tooth, she laughed even harder. "That's exactly what you get, toothless bitch!" She stood over the woman, anger and fury pouring down in the form of the spittle that dribbled from her open mouth.

The woman sobbed as her blood splattered on her dress.

Maggie whirled back to the woman's cart and grabbed the produce resting on the top of the heap. A few bananas, a head of lettuce, and a bag of potatoes were the easiest to grab. She picked them up and moved back in front of the woman. One at a time, she dropped the items on the woman's head. Each time one of them smacked her, she cried out but refused to look up at Maggie. Her aggression to regain her cart had fled in favor of fear.

Maggie returned to the cart and yanked a gallon of skim milk free from the bottom. She twisted the cap free and flicked it at the woman before returning to her. She stared down at the trembling woman without the slightest bit of remorse. Her anger was present but no longer rising like an ocean tide. She tilted the container over the woman until milk cascaded down to mix with the blood. The color of the two liquids blending together reminded Maggie of the fry sauce at Chick-fil-A. "Next time someone asks you to move your cart, find some fucking manners, and pull the damned thing out of the way." She dropped the milk container on the woman.

At the end of the aisle, a blonde lady and her small son rounded the corner. They stopped walking to stand and stare at the scene with their mouths hanging open.

The expressions on their faces had the effect of a thousand-pound weight falling on Maggie's head. A fog lifted from her mind, and she became aware of how different she had felt when the anger had overtaken her mind.

She glanced at the woman on the floor. The mess before her was more like something from a horror movie than a woman shopping for her groceries.

Maggie wanted to take it in objectively, as though she was simply observing what happened to the woman on the floor, in the same way as the blonde and her son did. That she had anything to do with the condition of the woman seemed ridiculous, but she was well aware of the damage she had inflicted. This was nothing she could see from a distance. It had been her doing. She had inflicted the damage that had turned another human being into a beaten dog.

A swell of emotion surged inside her and her breath hitched in her chest before the first tears in her eyes could fall. "Oh, my God, what have I done?"

"Leaf me alone…" The woman tilted onto the floor to lie in bloodied milk. She cried while holding her hands over her face.

"I didn't mean…I don't know…"

The blonde woman at the end of the aisle was busy digging in her purse, and Maggie knew she was desperately trying to find her phone. She was going to

Coming Up Short 9

call the police before Maggie could attack her and her child next. As Maggie gazed at them, the woman pulled her son behind her. "Stay away! Please!" Real fear had replaced the look of wonder on her face.

Maggie held out her hands. "I'm not...I mean I won't..."

The injured woman on the floor cried out, "You're a monshter!"

★★★

Maggie cried all the way home, fearful that flashing blue and red lights would soon come after her. She'd see them in her rearview mirror and have to pull over, which would lead to assault charges and jail time. Ultimately, Mark would leave her when he found out what a maniacal evil mess she'd become. "What have I done? What am I?" she asked herself as she turned off the main road to wind her way home through several neighborhoods. It would be better to avoid the cops and pray the store didn't have good security cameras. "I am a monster. She was right. I'm the worst kind of monster."

It wasn't until she arrived home and parked her car in the garage that she remembered to check the word, Qhar, pressed into the flesh of her finger. It was still there, though it had faded a little further. "Maybe Mark was right. Maybe that ring did something to me."

★★★

"Are you alright? You aren't eating much." Mark asked her between bites of dinner. He'd made tacos, which were her favorite, but she'd hardly touched her food, and she knew he'd notice.

While it was probably her guilt acting up, that he needed to point out the obvious about her appetite irritated her. She loved her husband, but he picked at every little thing sometimes. "I'm fine. Just had a rough day."

"Oh?" He set the remainder of a taco on his plate. The lettuce fell out of it, and he didn't notice. The half-empty taco shell bothered her. It was too much like her, only partially full of the things it needed to be complete. What bothered her even more was that Mark hadn't seen the displaced vegetables and replaced them in the shell. Maybe if he quit interrogating her, he could see the mess he'd made on his plate.

"Yeah, no biggie." She replied while trying to pry her eyes away from his mess.

"What happened? You seem upset." He stared at her.

Maggie stood from the table. "Oh, my God! Will you drop it!" She pushed her plate away. "I'll eat when I damn well please, and I don't need a reason for not being hungry. Got it?" She glared at him, her anger pounding in her eyes with the thudding of her heart.

"Jesus, Maggie! What's wrong with you?" Mark stood from the table and took his plate with him to the kitchen. "I've about had enough of your unreasonable anger. You need counseling."

Coming Up Short 9

The idea she was somehow mentally deficient and needed some idiot in a suit to tell her how messed up she was, was about the most insulting thing she could imagine Mark saying to her. She pushed to her feet, leaving her plate behind, and stomped into the kitchen. "Oh, is that so? So, Dr. Mark, mister used car finance guy, please tell me your professional diagnosis." She approached him where he stood at the sink. "Please, do tell me!"

Without giving her the courtesy of speaking to her face, he said, "I said you need counseling, because I'm not a professional, and clearly, I'm incapable of helping you. I don't know what's happened to you, but it needs to stop."

His words pissed her off. They were arrogant and self-righteous. His inability to acknowledge her as another adult and treat her with the decency of speaking to her face sent her over the edge. All semblance of being a reasonable person flew out the window like an escaping bird. She stepped forward and shoved Mark in the center of his back as hard as she could. Caught off guard, he jumped forward and slammed into the sink. "Ouch!"

"I'm such a shitty person now that you can't face me, is that it?" If she had a baseball bat, she'd hammer him in the head with it until he gained some damn sense.

Mark turned on her. "It's that print on your finger, Qhar, isn't it? This behavior isn't like you, Maggie. Can't you see what's happened to you? We need help with this." He reached for her hand, but she jerked away. "Let me see it."

Coming Up Short 9

"No." She backed away.

"I won't touch you but hold up your hand and let me see your finger." He demanded.

"No, you can't tell me what to do like you're some kind of big boss man. I'm your wife. You should show me some respect."

Mark rolled his eyes and laughed. "Yeah? Well, I'm not seeing a lot to respect." He smiled through the vexation plastered on his face. He did it to push her buttons further, and it worked.

Maggie could feel her cheeks flush, and the anger pour out of her. Before she could pull it back, her right hand slashed out and hit him across his smug face. Though she surprised herself, the loud clap her strike made felt good. It felt pure and righteous.

Maggie's attack only fazed Mark for a moment. He launched himself forward and wrapped his arms around her while pulling her tight against himself.

The air pushed from her lungs. "Let go of me!" she screeched at him.

"No! Not until you've got yourself settled down. This is absurd, so we're staying like this until you calm down."

She bucked in his arms, tried kicking his shins, and slammed her fists down onto his thighs. No matter what she did, she couldn't cause him enough pain to release her. "I hate you!" She tried making him feel guilty about imprisoning her, but it had no effect. He remained standing, his feet spread apart, his arms securely holding her against her will. She tried screaming and cursing at him. Instead of relenting, he only seemed to get stronger. After a few minutes, her body was tired, and the fight went out of her. Like a leaky balloon, the anger that had fueled her attack slowly escaped, leaving her limp and exhausted. As in the store, she felt overwhelmed by emotion.

After giving up her fight, she allowed herself to fall limp in his arms. He turned her so they were chest to chest and hugged her tight. His kindness and the love he showed her after all she'd done to him brought forth another round of tears. She wept against him while begging for his forgiveness.

"Can I see your finger, please?" He asked her again.

This time, she held up her hand without looking at it herself.

"Hmm. Still there, but mostly faded. I bet in a day or two it will be completely gone, and then we'll see if it's the cause of your personality changes."

"I just want to be okay." She whimpered.

"You will be, but if this mark in your skin fades and you're still struggling to manage your anger, we should get you an appointment to see someone."

She nodded against his chest. "Okay."

★★★

Coming Up Short 9

To Maggie, if Mark was right, and the word stamped on her finger was responsible for her sudden outbursts of anger, the reasonable thing to do was to go back to the jewelry store and ask Mr. Southerly about it. Maybe he had tried it on another customer who had a similar experience. It was a long shot, but maybe he'd be more forthcoming without Mark there to observe their conversation.

The good news was that the angst and anger permeating her being the night before seemed to have faded. She felt edgy, but not overly aggressive or ready to fight or beat a shopper to death in the supermarket.

After Mark was gone to work for the day, she'd drive the couple of miles to the downtown jewelry store. It had a funny name that she couldn't recall, but she knew exactly where to find it.

***

The bell over the door jingled as she entered The Netherworld Jewelry Store. As if she had only departed the store from her first visit a few minutes ago, Lived stood where she last saw him. He stood on the other side of the jewelry case where she had found the little gold ring with the large black stone.

"Welcome back, Maggie. I do hope you haven't come back for that ring. I sold it to a collector just last night, I'm afraid." His eyes twinkled and teased her. He was the man who always knew something others needed to know.

Maggie progressed across the wooden floor to the other side of the case and stood before Lived.

Coming Up Short 9

Sparkling blue eyes weren't his only charming asset. His mannerisms, so professional and yet personal with people, were disarming. His features were sharp, and like his eyes, they said he was young in spirit. He had to be at least seventy years old, but his energy and flare made her think he was much younger. He even appeared younger than the last time she'd seen him a few days before.

While she couldn't put her finger on it, there was a wisdom and strength about the old man she found fascinating. An energy existed under his façade. It was there, unseen, but there.

"No, I…well, I came in about the ring, but not to buy it." She said. He didn't respond to her, not exactly. His eyebrows twitched, and he smiled, but he didn't speak a word. She continued, unsure of why she had come back to his shop at all. "I, uh…"

"The ring." He reminded her. "You didn't want to buy it, but you came here about the ring." He offered a reassuring smile. "Are you having a bad day?"

The tension seemed to melt out of her. "I've had a few of them, yes, but thank you for reminding me. I'm not sure what's wrong with me lately. I…well, since that ring pressed Qhar into my flesh, I seem to be having some anger issues and that's not at all like me." She held up her ring finger to remind him of the impression the ring made on her skin.

"Yes, Qhar means angry in Dari." He smiled at her. "I apologize, Maggie. I don't mean to seem offensive, but…what are you trying to show me?"

Coming Up Short 9

"My finger. Remember the ring imprinted it into my skin?"

"Yes, I recall, but it's been well over a week, and it's gone." He nodded at her hand. "Your finger looks fine."

"Huh?" Maggie turned her hand so that she could see the skin on the top of her ring finger. Lived was right. It was blemish-free and looked like the rest of her hand. "It was there this morning."

"Well, these things tend to clear up at a moment's notice." Lived withdrew a set of keys from his pocket.

"I'm amazed. No wonder I feel better."

As he unlocked the cabinet with the antique jewelry, he asked her, "Do you?"

"Feel better?"

"Yes." He said without glancing up.

"I think so."

Lived removed a silver necklace from the case and laid it in on the glass countertop. "Was it Mark? Was he the source of your troubles?"

Maggie's eyes locked on the necklace. The silver sparkled under the artificial lighting of the store. A large clear jewel shined at its bottom. "Is that a diamond?"

"Yes, it is, but what about Mark?" He asked again.

She pulled her eyes away from the expensive antique. "I'm sorry, that beautiful piece distracted me. What did you ask about Mark?"

"Was he the factor causing you so much trouble?" His warm eyes found hers and she felt an instant connection. "If you'll excuse me for saying so, he seems the type of man to cause much angst and trouble."

Lived understood her. He was sympathetic, but more so, he was empathetic. He understood her situation and there weren't many people who did these days. She knew when she opened her mouth, it would all come pouring out. "Yes, Mark, he doesn't understand me, and he can be so infuriating." A daze came over her. It was a comforting one. She felt warm and fuzzy. She could stand in Lived's store talking to him all day. The memories of her recent anger came back to her, but she was no longer ashamed of them. Mark made her angry. It was his fault. If he wasn't such a bothersome ass, she would chill out.

Lived made a tsking sound and shook his head without shaking the glasses on his nose loose. "I'm not at all surprised. He seems that way, I guess. Although you shouldn't have to put up with it." At this, he made eye contact with her. "Don't you agree?" His blue eyes pulled her in.

She would agree with anything he said because he was wise and intelligent. More importantly, he was right. "Yes, I agree." Her mind returned her to the ring that had stamped a word into the flesh on her finger. It had made her feel...

"Angry?" Lived asked, and without allowing her to answer, said, "Yes, the ring made you angry, but, and this is important Maggie, it only brought out what was already inside of you. You should never deny those feelings. They're real and true. It's important that you acknowledge the deep emotions buried inside of you that the ring enhanced. Those are the same feelings Mark wants to keep you from. He doesn't understand you and never will." His disapproving glare said more than his words.

"I knew it." She felt lightheaded and embraced it. It wasn't a bad feeling, it was pleasant. Comfort came with knowledge. In that feeling of floating was the truth. Lived helped her find it. She didn't need to feel guilty about being angry. She had a right to the sentiment, and she had a right to be pissed off at Mark because he was the cause of most of it.

"You were right all along, Maggie." Lived encouraged her and the gleam in his eye told her she had his full support. "Far too often we are talked out of the things we feel, our emotions, and the subsequent actions we desire to take. But if you think about it, who is there to tell us what is right and wrong when we already know? What's right, and what's wrong, is for all of us to decide for ourselves. Why should we be subject to other's definitions of morality? You, Maggie, are perfectly capable of deciding how you feel for yourself." The words rolled off his tongue smoothly. He was intoxicating to listen to, and she would rather be nowhere else.

Coming Up Short 9

"That's how I felt in the grocery store with that rotten bitch and her damn cart." Recognition ignited inside of her. "And it's how I feel about Mark. He wants me to live by his rules, not mine." It all made sense finally, and she had the amazing old man to thank for the clarification. "I should leave him."

"Who, Mark?" He seemed surprised by her declaration.

"Yes, I should leave him. He's stifling me."

"Oh, I think you can do much better than leave him." He waved her forward. The flick of his fingers drawing her was subtle, but she saw it. "Come, try this on. I like you in that ring, but this necklace will be absolutely stunning on you."

Maggie stepped close to the case. Lived unclasped the necklace and invited her to lean forward. As she pulled her hair out of the way and bent toward him, Lived placed the necklace around her neck. As it passed her eyes, she realized the chain was much heavier and thicker than she had realized. Each interlocking component had to have been hand-crafted. It was amazing and lovely and far more expensive than she could ever afford.

Lived clasped the piece at the back of her neck and she allowed her hair to fall into place. The piece was warm against her flesh and instantly became a part of her. It was an extension of her being.

Lived was right, the necklace was gorgeous on her. She stared into a mirror that hung on the wall behind him. She was a new person, entirely. Lived had freed her spirit, and the necklace freed her beauty.

"Mark should treat you better. You deserve things like this, Maggie."

"Where did it come from?"

He grinned and winked at her. "Sixteenth century, England."

"Oh, my God!" The chain was heavy around her neck. It hugged both the back of her neck and her throat. If it was much tighter, she would struggle to breathe. Whoever had worn the piece in the past must have been a very slender woman. "Its original owner must have been royalty."

"Yes, indeed, Maggie. I'm not at liberty to disclose the identity of this woman to you because of a deal I made long ago, but she was indeed a very stern and powerful woman who wasn't afraid to stand her ground with men, even way back then."

His words affected her. He was right. She needed to be stronger. She needed to be like the version of herself who had beaten the bitch in the store, and she needed to be the woman who had stood up to Mark.

"Yes, that's right, Maggie. You need to be strong. Why shouldn't you be? A man who is lesser than you should never be allowed to control you like he has." He cooed to her from somewhere nearby, but she didn't see him. She could only see herself in the mirror. She grinned. Finding herself was much more of a discovery this morning than she anticipated.

Coming Up Short 9

"That woman in the store, you should have bashed her skull in for what she did. She certainly had it coming, behaving in such a rude manner." His voice floated to her and penetrated her mind.

"Yes, I should have kicked her teeth down her rotten throat and beat her head against the floor." The words came from her, but she didn't feel the out-of-control anger she felt before. Now she was in control and could be strong because of it.

"You will be strong. I guarantee it." He was as happy as she was. Lived sounded as though he was almost jumping for joy. As she grinned at herself in the mirror, the necklace tightened a bit around her neck. It was uncomfortable, but she could still breathe. "I love this, Lived."

Lived stepped back in front of her. As he moved, the necklace clamped down on her yet again. Unlike the previous time, she now felt herself struggling to get her air. "This is a little…" The skin on the back of her neck burned.

"Tight?" he nodded. "Yes, I see that." He said he saw it, but he didn't look at the necklace. Instead, his eyes searched hers. He was looking for her resolve. He wanted to know if she was a fighter.

"Help me!" She choked out.

"Let it do what it was created to do, Maggie." Lived seemed unconcerned.

Her hands found the necklace. She tried to slip her fingers under the front near the large stone, but the

Coming Up Short

band had dug far too deep into her flesh.
"Get...it...off..."

"You weren't wrong, Maggie. That woman in the store, Mark, the bitches at work who give you so much trouble, they're all wrong, and you're right. They deserve pain and they deserve death." He whispered to her and his voice now sounded much deeper, much darker. He was a powerful man who feared nothing and no one.

Her vision was fading. She resisted the overwhelming urge to collapse on the floor. She was strong, Lived was right about her and everyone else was wrong. They didn't believe in her, but they should.

Lived stared into her eyes. What he saw in them made his smile widen appreciably. He seemed pleased with her and reached out with a hand. He held it before her and snapped his fingers.

The necklace released itself and fell free of her neck. Before it could hit the counter, he snagged it out of the air and returned it to the case in one smooth movement.

She knew he shouldn't have been able to do what he did, but was grateful to get her air back. Breathing was more important than questioning.

Lived stood. "The necklace is an expensive piece, but sometimes we get lucky."

"What do you mean?" She asked.

Coming Up Short 9

"Sometimes the benefit of a thing doesn't come through ownership."

She agreed, "I don't need to own that necklace because it changed me, or you did." Her mind chewed on the subject of the old man. He was a mystery to her, and yet, there was something familiar about him. Even his name brought forth feelings of familiarity. "Your name, Lived. Is it possible I know you from before Mark and I came into your store?" She stepped back from the jewelry case as the lightheaded feeling faded.

Lived's voice was back to the smooth speaking voice she recalled from before. "My name? Well, sometimes what we see is all backward with what's real."

"Yes, backward." She nodded her understanding, although she couldn't define what he meant. It sounded right, but the truth in what he said was far away. "I better get going now. I'm going to buy a soda and head home."

Lived straightened his dark suit jacket. "If I might make a recommendation, I would suggest you grab one of those liquid death seltzer waters at a convenience store."

Maggie found herself standing at his closed shop door. "Oh, that's an odd name. Why do they call them that?"

Lived winked at her, his blue eyes shining brightly. "Why? Because they murder your thirst, of course."

Coming Up Short 9

"That's pretty creative marketing."

"It sure is."

"Goodbye Lived, thank you for…well, just thanks I guess…" She waved goodbye.

He returned the gesture and said, "You go have a murderous good time!"

"Huh?"

Lived turned away from her and entered a door at the rear of the store she hadn't noticed before. As he left the room, he said, "I'm referring to the beverage, of course."

★★★

Mark snored in the bed next to her. How he slept with her lamp on was a mystery to her. Not that she cared one way or another, she didn't. The truth was, she'd be better off without him. He was a demanding man who wanted to set her moral parameters, and she now understood, she didn't have to accommodate him.

Beyond his issues of control, she had other problems with him. Marrying him had been a mistake. In general, he was a useless man. She clicked off the TV and stared at him for a few moments. What she saw repulsed her. He was one of the people Lived had warned her about. There was nothing about him that was spectacular enough that she needed to spend the next forty years of her life doing his bidding.

Coming Up Short 9

As she stared at him, a peace came over her. It was a strange feeling because it was born in the idea she could kill him where he lay in their bed, and her life would improve dramatically. As Lived said, she had a duty to herself to be a strong woman and to eliminate those who tried to establish her code of ethics for her. What was right or wrong in her life was up to her, not Mark.

Killing him would be easy enough. She could do it so that he would never wake again. All it would take was to remove the lengthy pair of scissors from her nightstand drawer. She could slam them down into his temple before he could wake. She could tell the cops an intruder broke in and attacked them while they slept. It would be easy.

Lived had encouraged her to do it, and Lived was a wise man. He knew things that an ordinary person shouldn't. He was powerful. She could feel it in his presence.

She thought about the comment he'd made when they had spoken earlier in the day. She had asked about his name and commented on how unusual it was when he'd told her something she couldn't shake.

Sometimes what we see is all backward with what's real.

At the time, she'd been too taken and impressed with him to question his meaning.

Mark snored loudly and kicked out a leg, interrupting her thoughts. She used a foot to shove him back onto his side of the bed and returned to her

Coming Up Short

memory of Lived's answer about his name. It was the part he'd said about it being backward that she kept tripping over.

Sometimes what we see is all backward with what's real.

The elderly man had an unusual way about him, and he had an unusual way of speaking.

Maggie contemplated his answer to her question. She had asked him why his name seemed familiar, and he answered by telling her that sometimes things were backward.

She clicked off her light and lay back on the bed. Using her mind's eye, she replayed the conversation one last time.

If his backward comment was about his name, maybe she should say it backward for once.

She arranged the letters of his name in reverse order in her head.

"D.E.V.I.L."

She fell still for a moment while she checked her spelling. She had it correct. Lived was backward, as he'd said.

In the dark, Maggie smiled. Though no one was awake to notice, she could feel it and it felt good. It was high time she was allowed to feel good after all Mark had

Coming Up Short

done to diminish her. He'd been the concrete blocks tied to her ankles. She had been correct. Mark needed to go.

And she'd been right about one more thing.

There was something special about the old man in the jewelry store.

★★★

Maggie lay still on the other half of the bed and that was a good thing. She'd been under a tremendous amount of stress lately and the sleep would do her good. It was what she needed. Maybe a large part of her recent stress was related to a lack of solid rest. He contemplated kissing her forehead, but didn't want to wake her. She'd been through a lot lately.

Mark kicked his legs over the edge of the bed, his urge to pee more than adequate enough to drive him from the warmth of the covers. He had an issue with not drinking enough water during the day, over-drinking at night, and then waking up to run to the bathroom. Though he'd promised himself over and over to remember to drink more water during the day, he still hadn't gotten it done.

In the past, Maggie had complained to him that his getting up and down woke her, but this time, she didn't move. She must truly have been on the edge of exhaustion.

He padded his way across their bedroom to the master bath, slipped inside, and closed the door. Careful to make sure he made no noise; he tiptoed across the cold tile floors to the toilet. The room was chilly, but

Coming Up Short 9

that's what sleeping in only a pair of boxers would get him in the night.

His mind reverted to the issues with Maggie while he did his business. A week ago, she had been completely normal, and while he'd never be able to prove anything, the changes in her had come from the moment they'd stepped into the small antique jewelry store. Their visit had been a strange one and Maggie had started picking at him that day.

It was because of the damn ring. It had to have been, although, a quick peek at her finger earlier in the evening had given him much relief. The little print of the Dari word on her finger was gone, and what had been even more promising was her nasty disposition of the previous several days seemed to be gone as well. While she hadn't been overly jubilant, or kind, and maybe she'd even been a little distant, the snarky bickering he'd been living with was notably absent.

It was weird to think about, but maybe that old ring carried some sort of curse or something. He'd go back and ask the old store owner, but the only thing creepier than what had happened to Maggie was the old man. There was something wrong with him.

Eventually, he'd read an article in the local paper about the old man killing someone in his store or something equally evil and he'd be able to tell Maggie he'd been right about the old geezer.

After flushing the toilet and washing up, Mark returned to the bathroom door. He could get three more hours of sleep before he needed to be up for work, and he wanted them all. He eased the door open. Staring into the dark bedroom, he recognized the flash of Maggie's white nightgown coming at him.

She was running and his intuition was that she was sick, and he needed to move out of the way so she could make it to the toilet in time.

As he stepped aside, though, she course-corrected herself and hit him straight in the chest. Her momentum carried them both over and he landed in a heap on the bathroom floor with her parked on his chest.

"What the hell, Maggie?" She'd done it on purpose. He'd seen her alter her route into the bathroom to collide with him, and now she squatted over him, snickering about her accomplishment. "I don't see anything that's funny! That shit hurt!"

She leaned closer to him. With her new position, he saw her face more clearly. The person staring down at him was his wife, and she wasn't. Though it was Maggie parked on him, her face was twisted into a filthy mask of anger.

With her sitting on his crotch, he had a distant and random thought she was surprising him with some aggressive and unusual sex, but the way her face made her look like a rage-filled old man shoved the thought out of his head.

She giggled at him. Her mouth opened and for the slightest moment, he thought he saw fangs in the corners of her mouth. She spoke to him through a giggle that implied she knew she wasn't funny and that was her entire point, to be anything but funny. "If you thought that hurt, we'll see how you feel after this!"

Her arm flashed down, and an immense pain bloomed in his chest. His heart hitched in his chest. It stayed beating but in an atypical rhythm. It clunked in his chest and warm blood leaked down onto his neck.

"What…" He wanted to question her and ask why she had hurt him. He also wanted her off his chest and waist. He couldn't breathe and his energy was beginning to wane. Getting his words out seemed an impossible task. Though he told his arms to toss her aside, they remained lying at his sides. His legs were uncooperative and only flinched when he willed them to move.

"You useless asshole!" Maggie seethed at him through clenched teeth. "I never really liked you; did you know that? Wasn't it obvious to you, Mark, that I grew tired of your constant control? That early pregnancy scare we had was the reason I married you. If I had known then that it was only a false alarm, I would have laughed in your face when you proposed." She rolled her eyes. "And for the record, before you die, I want you to know that I hate your mother, too. The nosey old wench, when I'm done with you, I should go to her house and take care of her too." She giggled. "That would make my night perfect." She extended the last word to add emphasis to her claim that the death of his mother would only make things better.

"Mags…" She was out of her mind, and if she didn't get him help, he was going to die.

Coming Up Short 9

The shot of adrenaline at the thought of his death only caused his heart to struggle more. Things were going south very quickly, and time was evaporating.

"Mags!" she screeched. "See? That right there is why this needed to happen. You're just as big a control freak as Lived said you are, and oh boy, do I know a big secret about him!" She squealed and rolled side to side. Her eyes found his. "You spent years trying to tell me what to do about everything and I'm sick of it! And calling me Mags, or Magpie, through the years after all the times I told you my name was Maggie, only made things worse!" She pounded a fist against his chest. "You're an arrogant bastard!"

Maggie slid off his chest and the relief he anticipated with the removal of her weight did not come. He still felt like a Chevy truck was parked on him.

She sat on her butt with her knees drawn up to her chest, facing away from him. "Lived was right. All along, he was so right." She placed her head in her hands and leaned forward. She laughed as she yelled into the bedroom. "I'll finally get a good night's rest without you waking me up every hour too! This is the greatest feeling in the entire world!"

She leaned forward to stand, and her long hair split in the middle to fall over her shoulders, exposing the back of her neck.

Mark stared at the skin there, amazed at the little red irritated patch his eyes found. In the center of the redness was a single word.

Coming Up Short 9

"Queller…" He recalled the word from a Seventeenth Century European studies class he'd had in college. It was an Old English word. Its meaning was close, floating out of reach in his fading mind.

Maggie stood and flipped her hair behind her. "What honey, dearest? Your voice is just too quiet to hear now. I suspect it's because you're dying." Her eyes darted around him. "Wow! If you could see it, you'd be amazed at the amount of blood on the floor. I'm surprised you have any left inside of you."

His memory clicked into place, and the definition of Queller followed. "It…it means…killer." He tried to tell her. The word on her neck meant she'd been back to the jewelry store. The old man had done it to her again. "Evil…" He uttered as the darkness narrowed his vision to a single point. All that remained of his earthly sight was a small image of Maggie staring down at him. His heart tripped out a last few beats and then stilled.

"Yes, he is, Mark. He's the devil."

Coming Up Short 9

KoK

The woman he followed from the bar was one of the better-looking that he and Ace had approached. Of course, Ace had struck out with her. That much was expected. The skill his friend had in the world of violence and depravity was overshadowed by his inadequacy around women. It was why he hated the fairer sex as he did.

Ace wasn't usually the lead in these situations, but tonight, he decided to have some additional fun. It had been hilarious to watch Ace fall flat on his face as he'd tried to flirt his way into getting the woman to leave the bar with him.

As was normally the case, Ace had failed, but he, being a thinking man, had not. After a few minutes of speaking to the uppity bitch, he'd figured out she was only there to prick-tease men, which had changed his strategy entirely. Instead of continuing to flirt with her, he had gone in a different direction. He'd stayed as close to her as possible, speaking non-stop about weird things, in strange ways, until she had finally stood, looked him up and down, and said, "This place is fucked. Where are all the good men? I'm out of here. What a jerk!"

He had laughed when she'd said it. He couldn't help himself. She was so full of herself that she thought by declaring her intention to leave, she could be rid of him.

Coming Up Short 9

Her thought had been wrong, and a blatant case of tragically misplaced arrogance to believe she could dismiss him so easily.

Now, he followed her out of the bar, keeping to the shadows at the edge of the building. He placed light steps on the damp concrete and felt his excitement rise tremendously when she turned into the alley next to the inner-city bar.

Ace and his leather bomber jacket wouldn't be far behind him. The man always wore his jacket to the bar. He thought women liked it. He was wrong, but Ace had his redeeming qualities. The things he could do to a woman's body after she was dead were truly works of art.

He turned the corner, and after making sure the dark alley was without sleeping bums or anyone else hiding in the shadows, hurried to the woman and placed a hand on her shoulder. She whirled around and glared at him. "What the fuck, dude? I told you to piss off. Why are you following me?"

The rage in him boiled over. She was the type of woman who diminished men everywhere she went, and it was time for her to understand there were consequences for such actions.

As he stared into her eyes, he saw fear creep in to replace the bravado she displayed. Seeing that little bit of terror was a huge turn-on. Her control was slipping, and she knew it.

"What do you want? First that dipshit Ace, and now you…men are all pigs! I swear I'll scream if you…"

Coming Up Short 9

He flashed forward and clutched her neck in both hands.

The feel of her tender flesh excited him. There was no way he would hold off until Ace arrived in the alley, which was alright. Ace preferred them dead, anyway.

★★★

The random images crashed through his head, but he was prepared for them. They'd been coming faster and faster over the past few days.

He knew he was hiding in the shadows at the side of a 7-11, waiting for a white Chevrolet Malibu to pull up to the gas pumps. The driver, a middle-aged man, would soon arrive, exit, and go into the store. That's when he'd make his first move.

He had it all planned out based on the things he'd seen in his head, and he'd made the trip to the location ready to act on his plans. Unfortunately, the erratic scenes came when they wanted. And now, as he stood in hiding, one of those random visions arrived. There was no way to shake it off and no way to see anything other than the coming scene of violence. He had no choice but to play the part of the silent observer.

With his eyes clamped shut, the fragments of a picture, like a jigsaw puzzle, jumbled up and slid together to form an image that would soon become a motion picture.

Like having a private movie theater in his head, a movie clip would play for him, and he'd pay as close attention as possible. The little advanced peeks provided him with all he needed to know. They always lead him to where he would need to go; the next murder.

Inside his head, a scene came in which a man wearing a long overcoat moved into an alley behind a woman. He had no stomachache, which meant what he was about to see, the murder he'd witness had already happened. The killing that was coming was past tense. He'd see it as it had happened, but there was nothing he could do about it.

The bottom of the man's coat flapped in a slight breeze. A distant overhead streetlight provided the only light he saw inside his mind. The woman, tall, blonde, and thin, walked with an angry gait, each step threatening to bust off one of her lengthy heels. Her ankles flexed with each step, and he knew she was scared and upset. He could also tell in his limited advanced sight; she was unaware of the man who followed her.

Her pursuer walked lightly and, in time, with her steps. He didn't want to be revealed yet.

No, not yet, but soon…your excitement is building. You're almost close enough to touch her and it's the moment she sees you and terror comes into her eyes, that you live for, isn't it? It's your addiction and you'll never live without it.

The woman hesitated at the edge of a deep shadow, much like the one he hid in, before turning and coming face to face with the man in the long overcoat. Her eyes widened and her mouth opened. "What the hell? I told you to piss off. Why are you following me?"

Coming Up Short 9

  The movie continued to flash inside his mind, and he was completely unaware of the things that went on around him. He needed the vision to complete so he could be ready for the arrival of the white Malibu. Though he had no control over when the visions came to him, what they contained, or how long they consumed his mind's eye, he knew he would soon need to rejoin the present.

  On the movie screen in his head, the man in the overcoat chuckled and the woman, in her sparkling red dress, stepped back from him. "What do you want? First dipshit Ace, and now you…men are all pigs! I swear I'll scream if you…"

  The excitement within the man in the coat built until he was ready to explode. He lashed both hands out at the woman and wrapped them around her slender, white throat. Her eyes bulged, and she tried to cough. She wanted to plead with him for her life and she deeply desired to breathe, but she could do none of these things. He lifted her until her feet left the oily asphalt surface of the alley. As she kicked, one of her heels flew off her foot.

  You're in your element now. This is what you crave. You want to stare into her eyes as her life is extinguished. I know this, and I know you. I know all about you without knowing you because I'm just like you. That's right, you don't know me yet, but you soon will. And when that time comes, it will be my turn for some fun.

  Piss dribbled down the woman's legs as her bladder let go and the spark and fury she used to batter the man's arms abated. She was losing her fight. Her body slumped as her spirit abandoned her body and the man leaned close to her. He sniffed her hair and placed his lips against her damp cheek.

Sounds from the world around him returned and the image of the woman being choked to death in his mind broke apart. It shattered into a million pieces before fading for good. What he had seen was done. There was nothing he could do to save the woman. Her murder had already taken place, but what he would soon see, the visions yet to come, would be about what was yet to happen. He'd know them by the gut-wrenching pain he'd feel when he slipped into that other place. It was how it always played out, and those scenes represented the chance he had to save someone and redeem himself. He supposed that was why he had been given such a gift.

He opened his eyes in time to see a white car as it approached the gas station island. It was the only car in the lot. At this time of night, fuel seekers were few and far between, making what he needed to do much easier.

He tried to force the nasty remains of the scene from his head and focused on the car. One thought lingered with him, though. The vision was troubling because it was unfamiliar. The killer he pursued had always worn the long overcoat, but he had never seen him killing a woman in an alley before. Up to this point, the killer had always entered a home through an unlocked sliding glass door.

That's the first time I've seen this go in that direction.

Coming Up Short 9

Brake lights came on and the car rolled to a stop. The engine turned off, and the driver's door opened. In the artificial light of the gas pumps, he saw the man was the same pudgy, balding man he'd seen previously in other visions. And as anticipated, the man hurried around his car to the pump. He wore tan slacks and a soft blue shirt. He'd gotten off work late and wanted to go home but needed fuel to get there. On his way home, would the man slide, unnoticed, through a glass door to kill?

Maybe, but these things, these little films I get in my head, can be deceiving. He may not be the guy I want, and then again, in the end, he might be the one who wears the long coat.

With the fuel nozzle in the port on his car and filling his gas tank, the man left the fuel pump island to enter the store. He would buy something, a candy bar if the dreams had been correct, and he'd come back outside.

Time was short.

★★★

"Excuse me, sir…" He approached the man in the tan slacks and light blue shirt as he finished filling the Chevy's gas tank. He had indeed run into the store for the candy bar. It was a snickers he had been after and he'd already consumed it before reaching his fueling car. The older man replaced the nozzle on the gas pump.

As he approached his target, with his right hand in his jacket pocket, he felt the cold metal of the Berretta. It was silenced and ready to be triggered at a moment's notice.

Coming Up Short 9

The man at the pump pivoted to glance at him. With his hoodie intentionally pulled over his head, he hoped to limit the security camera's ability to identify him. If everything went according to plan, it wouldn't matter, but a good motto was - better safe than sorry.

"Yeah?" The bald man straightened from the gas pump and shifted his feet so that he faced him.

Stepping to within two feet of the man allowed him to use his body as a shield. The lone 7-11 employee inside the store wouldn't see his face or his weapon if he needed to pull it. He smiled at the bald man, unsure if he was about to scare the hell out of a regular guy with no harmful intentions, or if he was facing a monster. He spoke to him, positive the man was the former, not the latter. "I'm going to cut to the chase."

The man's forehead wrinkled with worry lines. "Yes? About what?"

"In my pocket I've got a 9-millimeter gun trained on the center of your chest. I know this will be upsetting to hear, but we're going to jump in your car and take a drive." He tugged the handle of the weapon free of his pocket just enough.

The man saw it. He did his best to not show the reaction he felt all the way from his head to his toes. His glance at the person working inside the store didn't go unnoticed. "Don't do anything to gain his attention or you'll put both of you at risk unnecessarily." Though he hated his approach, it was only based on his lack of knowledge of the man. Was the older man related to a victim? Was he a coming victim? Or was he the demon who needed to be dispatched back into the depths of hell?

"Look…" the man raised his hands.

"Put them down. We're going to play this cool. You'll understand shortly." He nodded to the car. "I want you to open the passenger door and then go around to the driver's door. We'll get into the car together. Understand?"

"Are you going to carjack me?" The man's complexion had fallen to a pale white. He appeared to wear ghost makeup in anticipation of a Halloween party.

Carjack? Isn't that where someone steals your car?

"Around the car, now." He kept his voice even but full of warning.

"Okay, okay. Take it easy." The man turned away and opened the passenger door. He then scurried around the rear of the sedan and approached the driver's door with one last longing stare into the 7-11.

"Get inside." He waited until the man bent down and had most of himself in the driver's seat before climbing into the passenger seat. He kept his door open and his right hand on the trigger of his weapon. "Shut your door."

"Listen," the man had his hands on the steering wheel at ten and two. He spoke with a nervous quiver in his voice. The slight jowls hanging from his jaw jiggled as he moved. "If it's money you're after, I, well we, don't have much, but I can give you what we got. I'm a giving person. You don't need that gun to get me to help you."

Guilt climbed into his consciousness, but he shoved it away. It could all be an act by the man to get him to drop his guard. "This isn't about money. Shut your door."

The man acquiesced. As soon as it clicked shut, he pulled his door closed as well. "Start it, but don't drive anywhere yet."

The man kept his gaze straight ahead but cranked the key. The engine turned over and started. He asked, "Will you tell me what you want if this isn't about money?"

The rumble from the front of the car meant things were progressing as he hoped they would. He thought back to the images that had previously taken ownership of his conscious mind. The gory visuals that had come to him repeatedly, as they typically did. Most depicted a man in an overcoat shooting a red-headed woman in the head as she knelt before him. Next to her, also on their knees, her family screamed and wailed. One was a man, her husband; his face too fuzzy to see and the other was a daughter. She was also not clear enough in the scene to identify.

The mother, dead before she hit the tiled kitchen floor, toppled toward the daughter. Her loving daughter screamed until her eyes rolled back in her head. The man, the killer in the overcoat, was the last part of the film that he'd seen in his head. What he'd seen had not yet happened, but it would.

Coming Up Short 9

The evil bastard in the vision held the weapon in his left hand. One prominent clue he saw before the image collapsed in on itself was a cartoon tiger, much like the one named Tony in the old cereal commercials. It came in the form of a tattoo on the base of the killer's exposed thumb. This was important because, like the victims, he had never gotten a clear view of the killer's face.

The scene would soon play out in reality, which created the pressure he felt to hurry this man along. The question was, who was this man quivering in the driver's seat? He only knew he was somehow involved in the violence that was to come. He'd seen the white car at the 7-11 in several other visions and had eventually determined the date and time he needed to be there.

"Hold up both of your hands so I can see your thumbs." He demanded.

The man released the steering wheel and turned his hands over. He had no tattoos anywhere on either hand.

Well, that didn't help.

"Do you have any tiger tattoos?" He asked.

"No, I don't have any tattoos at all."

Out of curiosity, he asked, "Why not?"

"I don't like them." The man said, his voice still shaky. His eyes grew large in his head, and he added, "For me, I mean. I like them fine. I just never wanted one. I didn't mean to offend, if you have any."

Coming Up Short 9

"Honestly, I feel the same way. I never understood the desire to inject ink into your skin." He asked the man, "What's your name?"

"It's Darren. And my wife and daughter are waiting for me. If I don't show up, they'll call the cops."

He turned in his seat and withdrew the gun from his pocket. "Wife and daughter?"

The man nodded his head. "Yes."

"How old's your daughter?"

The man risked a glance in his direction. "She's got nothing to do with this. You just get her out of your head."

"I don't want to hurt her. How old is she?" He repeated.

"Sixteen, but…"

"Your wife, is she a redhead?"

Darren turned to stare at him, his mouth hanging open in a tight little O-shape. "How'd you know that?"

It's them. The two from my vision. This man is the husband who was on his knees.

"Do you know anyone named Ace?"

Darren shook his head. "No, I swear it."

Coming Up Short 9

"Darren, this is going to be difficult to believe, but you need to do something." He said, the anger in him building.

"What?" A trickle of sweat dropped from the driver's forehead to stain his blue shirt.

"We have to get to your house, and we need to get there fast. You need to drive there now!"

The man didn't move a muscle. "I'd rather you kill me than take you to my house to harm my family. I won't do it." Air whistled out of Darren's nose as he clamped his jaw shut, determined to protect his family.

He sighed and slipped the gun back into his pocket. "Look, I'm putting the gun back so you can see I don't intend to harm you or your family. Someone very bad is coming and if you don't get me to your house, they're going to die."

Darren scowled at him. "How do you know this?"

"I saw it." He stared into Darren's eyes. "If you choose not to believe me, they'll die."

Darren stared back at him. "Who are you? What's your name?"

Without wasting a precious second, he answered, "My name's Kalen, and I'm here to help you. Now get a move on, or we'll soon be having a very different conversation." He grabbed Darren's arm. "Come on, man, your family doesn't have much time."

Coming Up Short 9

★★★

"You can look at me when we speak but do it after we get to your house." Kalen needed to get the man to understand he was on his side. "You don't need to fear me, you need to fear what's coming."

Of course, he's not looking in my direction because he thinks it'll help if he can convince me he hasn't seen enough of me to ID me.

"Why not call the cops?" Darren asked.

The way he proposed the question was without weight, like it was a casual thing for him to mention. He was trying to buy time.

And I know why...

"They'll never get there in time. And you're heading toward the police station as we speak, but again, the choices you make over the next few minutes will decide if your family lives or dies. It's your choice."

"Dammit!" Darren smacked the steering wheel with the heel of his hand. "You're going to kill someone at my house tonight!"

Kalen shrugged. "I know this is hard, but the wheels have already been set in motion, quite literally I'm afraid. Someone's going to die tonight. Who that is, is up to you, Darren. I won't harm a hair on your wife or daughter's heads, but the deviant, sneaky fuck who's coming for them will. It's his plan. The more of his kind that perish, the safer we all are, the safer our families are. Do you understand?"

Coming Up Short 9

"You've done this before, haven't you?" he held up a hand. "Wait! Don't answer that. I don't want to know."

"The answer is yes. I know what I'm doing."

"Shit!" Darren yanked the wheel left in an intersection and deviated from his intended path. "If you're lying to me and I just got my wife and daughter killed…I'll…I don't know, but I'll kill you!" Darren glanced at him and opened his eyes exaggeratedly.

Kalen smiled. He couldn't help it. People were funny when they panicked.

"I don't see the humor in any of this!" Darren yelled.

"I know you don't."

"How can you sit there so damn calm?" Darren cut off a mini-van switching lanes and earned a series of honks and curses.

"I know I need to be centered and stymie my anger at these moments. Inside, I'm all boiling rage. I've had killers come after me and my family before, so I know how you feel. Years ago, I lost my precious sister Abby to a murdering prick. Believe me when I say I've been in your shoes, only there was no one there to help me." Kalen noted how rigidly Darren held onto the steering wheel. The man's knuckles were white with the strain.

He's going to be sore for days.

Coming Up Short 9

Darren snorted.

"What?" Kalen asked.

"I'll be thankful for your help if you're telling the truth."

Kalen eyed him. "Why wouldn't I be?"

"Anyone could claim they intended to help in this situation and say my family is in peril so that he could kill us all and steal us blind." Darren whipped the car around another corner, this time into a residential neighborhood.

"It's a good thing that I'm telling the truth then, isn't it?"

Ignoring his comment and question, Darren asked, "Can I call my wife and prepare her?"

Kalen shook his head. "Are you kidding me?"

"What?" Darren complained.

"Great idea, and let's ask her to call the cops while we're at it," Kalen mocked him.

"We should have from the beginning." Darren insisted.

"When this is all done, you'll see that I'm right."

Coming Up Short 9

Darren leaned toward the steering wheel to stretch his back as he approached a stop sign. "Why?"

Kalen, with his voice flat and honest, answered, "Because when they come to get you in your own home, it's usually someone you know."

Darren said nothing as he guided his car up a residential street. Speaking was unnecessary. How he felt about the circumstances could be seen in the buckets of sweat pouring down his face.

We're close. I can see it in his stare. He's scared to death, and he should be.

★★★

Darren steered the car expertly down another street. While the car moved along, Kalen closed his eyes against a coming vision.

Here we go again.

Things would soon reach a conclusion. When the brief scenes in his head started coming faster, usually, he was on the verge of completing whatever mission had been thrust upon him. Kalen waited as the darkness in his mind cleared to create a cloudy scene.

Images in his head coalesced into one solid scene. He observed several people, mostly couples, inside a dark bar. Everyone had a drink on their tables. Loud music blared from overhead speakers, forcing the couples all to yell at each other to communicate. Those who had been together for only a little while used the loud sound as an excuse to lean close to their lovers and whisper in their ears.

As though an invisible cameraman angled through the bar, Kalen observed the scene, never sure of what he should pay close attention to next. The movement of his movie screen seemed to slow. Ahead, a man and woman sat side by side at a small table. The woman smiled as she stirred her drink with her straw. Her black top and skirt nicely complimented her long blonde hair. The man had his back to Kalen, but he wore the long overcoat he had become accustomed to seeing.

The woman smiled (she was flirting – it was subtle, but there) and slipped from her stool. She stumbled for a moment and the man in the long coat clutched her arm, lending stability. Above the music, Kalen heard the man tell her to be careful.

She responded with a promise to do exactly that and then excused herself to the lady's room.

As she walked away, Kalen observed the man fumble in a coat pocket and then withdraw a small glass vial with clear liquid in it.

You sneaky little shit.

The man scanned the surrounding crowd to make sure no one was paying attention, and then quickly reached up and dumped the contents of the vial into his date's cocktail. She was drinking something colored neon blue. It reminded Kalen of vacationing somewhere tropical. The additional substance in the drink didn't change its appearance at all. More than likely, its taste wouldn't be affected either.

The man tapped the vial against the rim of her glass to ensure all its contents dribbled into the drink, and then he tucked it away again.

Kalen's view of the man tilted to the right. His gut twisted and formed a tight knot.

This hasn't happened yet.

He hoped for a view of the pervert's face, but only got a look at the T-shirt he wore under his coat. A cartoon character of a pompous bird was featured surrounded by a series of words.

Foghorn Leghorn? Jesus, women today will go out with anyone.

Kalen read the words, and inside his own mind, rolled his eyes.

I say, I say, boy...I'm going to let God fix it. If I fix it, I'm going to jail.

Kalen snickered to himself.

This would have been great advice for me years ago, but oh well, it's far too late for that now. And my message to you, you secretive little prick, is this – there truly won't be any jail for you, but believe me when I say, if you knew what was coming, you'd beg for it.

Coming Up Short 9

The woman returned from the restroom. The way her hips shifted as she approached the table would intoxicate most men in the place. Her date shifted on his stool, making room for her to return to her seat.

"You were fast." He said as he moved. His voice, low and grainy, was as Kalen anticipated.

"Thanks, Brian. I got lucky; the restroom was unoccupied." She smiled as she sat.

Brian...

Kalen prayed his movie screen would shift. One little peek at the man's face would be of significant help. So far, the long coat was present as it had been in each of the previous visions.

The woman picked up her drink and held it close to her mouth as she spoke.

Don't drink it, lady.

As her drink came closer to her cherry-red lips, and she winked over the rim of her cup at the man who wanted to rape and kill her, Kalen's view twisted and morphed into cloudy, inky sludge. It was as though his movie screen melted under the intense heat of a million suns. The man in the long overcoat dissolved along with the woman he intended to drug. The bar and other customers also converged into a mixed-up mess of humanity and real estate. Colors converged until his movie screen was a swirling mass of confusion.

What the hell is this?

Coming Up Short 9

Out of the murk, a new scene came into view. It formed from the churning gray into a moving picture comprised of color and sound. Around a tan pair of slacks and black boots, the bottom of a long dark overcoat swirled. It flapped around the man wearing it like a bat, free from its cave to fly in the cool night air.

Why am I seeing you in a new place?

Kalen's camera man brought the angle of his view up until the murderer in the overcoat moved away and around the corner of a house. As he moved, he spoke to the night, "I'm coming for you, Missy. You bitches will see what I'm all about now."

The coat fluttered as a shadow consumed him. The movie screen shifted away from the disappearing man. Kalen saw the flash of a house. An address plaque, mounted on the corner of a double-car garage, showed four numbers.

In his mind, Kalen leaned as far forward as possible to see through the murk.

One, one, two, one. This is the address of where the man will head tonight, and I bet I know who lives there.

As though he were being yanked through solid walls made of wood and metal, Kalen surged forward, through the garage wall, in and out of temporary darkness, in time to stand before a sliding glass door. Though vertical blinds covered it, he knew it would soon slide open.

It'll be him, just like in the visions before.

Coming Up Short 9

The scene in his head evaporated. His clenching stomach began to settle and relax. Next to him, in the driver's seat, Darren asked, "Did you hear me? What happens when we get to my house?"

"What's your house number?"

Darren clenched the steering wheel harder. "That doesn't matter. I'm taking you there now."

"Is it one one two one?"

"How'd you know that?" Darren pressed, sounding angry. "Have you been stalking me?"

"I told you I see things." Kalen urged him forward. "Hurry, we don't have much time."

His reaction says I was right. The piece of shit is coming after Darren's family.

Darren turned to glance at him. "See things how?"

"In my head. Now focus on the road."

Darren hammered the horn as a teenage kid almost stepped in front of his Chevy.

"Who do you know that wears a long trench coat over T-shirts with cartoon characters on them?" Kalen asked.

Though he wanted to roll his eyes, Darren answered, "The only guy I know who would wear anything like that is Jimmy."

"Who's Jimmy?"

"Our idiot neighbor, but I don't know much about him. He's a loner. Keeps to himself mostly other than to bitch at my wife and kid from time to time. Why are you asking me about him?" Darren turned a corner on what felt like two wheels and continued down another lengthy street.

Kalen continued with his questions. There was limited time to get the answers he needed. "His name isn't Brian?"

Darren shook his head from side to side. "No, I don't know a Brian."

"Damn, okay, drive faster."

Darren slowed the car and yanked the wheel to the left. "We're here." He pointed through the windshield to a house at the end of a cul-de-sac. The Chevy's headlights illuminated a white ranch-style home with a two-car garage. "It's right there."

It's the house from my visions. They're never wrong.

"Pull in like you normally would. Where do you usually park?"

Coming Up Short 9

"In the driveway," Darren answered. He was wound tight; his face crumpled with stress and worry. His lips pressed tightly together.

"Pull in and shut off the car. Do not get out until I'm outside and standing in front of the car. Do you understand?"

"Yes."

Darren slid the car to a stop in the driveway and shut off the car.

"Give me the keys." Kalen held out his left hand.

"Why?"

"I like you Darren, but you're not too sure about me yet. Let's leave it at that." He kept his hand extended, palm up, waiting. "Come on, time's wasting."

"Please don't hurt my family, okay? They're all I've got." Darren pulled the car keys free of the ignition and placed them in Kalen's hand.

Kalen opened his door. On his way out of the car, he said, "You've got my word."

★★★

They were no more than inside the house, standing in a hallway, when Darren's wife called out to him. "Hi, honey! We're back here watching a movie, and I've got dinner ready. Oh, and we're free of Eddie for the evening. He's out bar hopping again, I think. You know how he is; he doesn't say much when he leaves."

At the sound of his wife's voice, Darren stepped forward, hurrying to get to her.

Kalen grabbed Darren, who stood a full foot shorter than him by the collar and yanked him to a stop. "Who's Eddie?"

Darren whispered. "He's my wife's idiot, delinquent nephew who's far too busy chasing after skirts to get a job. He lives in our basement, but you heard her. He's not here."

"Why didn't you tell me about him?" Kalen spoke while keeping an eye on the end of the hall, where the flickering light of a TV was the only illumination against pervasive darkness.

"I forget about him. We don't see much of him these days. His living here was supposed to be temporary, maybe a couple of weeks, but it's already been six months. Sarah gets upset when I tell her he needs to leave, so I guess I've learned to ignore the situation."

"Sarah is your wife?"

"Yes."

"Is your daughter here?"

Darren pointed down the hall. "She should be with my wife."

Coming Up Short 9

"What's her name?"

"Missy."

Kalen flashed back to his most recent vision. The killer in the overcoat's words bounded through his head.

I'm coming for you, Missy. You bitches will see what I'm all about now.

"Alright, let's go." Kalen pushed Darren forward and released his shirt.

Kalen followed Darren into the living room, where the TV flashed bright images of a couple playing on the beach. Only the undercurrent of dark music forecast the terrible things coming for them. The room was long and somewhat narrow. Painted in a light shade of gray, it featured a variety of family-oriented wall hangings and culminated in a fireplace at its end. Across from them, a series of vertical blinds covered what undoubtedly was the sliding glass door from his visions.

Without turning, a redheaded woman who sat on a lengthy sofa said, "We're almost done with this movie your daughter talked me into. This man and his wife are on vacation and…"

"Mom!" A teenage girl, red-headed like her mother, stared at Kalen where he stood behind her father. She sat on the other side of the room from her mother on an over-stuffed chair, her legs tucked under her.

"Oh, I'm not going to ruin it!" complained her mother, who had still not turned around. "We both know how this is going to end. That rotten captain guy isn't really dead, and he's going to come back and start the damned love triangle all over again."

"No, Mom..." The girl used a remote to mute the TV and stood from her chair. Her eyes locked on Kalen. She was suspicious of him, probably because of the look of panic and dread on her father's face.

Though Kalen couldn't see Darren other than from behind, he could guess at the stare he was giving his daughter. It would be a look of warning. Keep your mouth shut and do as you're told.

Finally, the middle-aged woman on the sofa stood to see what had so captivated her daughter's attention. Her eyes shifted from Darren to Kalen and back to Darren. "Oh, geez, where are our manners? I don't recall you saying you were bringing a friend home tonight, hon..." She searched her husband's face for an explanation. "Darren?"

"Honey, we don't have much time..." Darren began, his voice cracking twice.

Missy, their daughter, placed a hand over her mouth as her tears began to fall. "Daddy? What's going on?"

"It's going to be okay, but we have to do what this man tells us, okay? We're in danger and..."

"Do you have a gun in that jacket?" Sarah asked Kalen.

Kalen cleared his throat.

Coming Up Short 9

You couldn't have messed that up more if you tried, Darren.

"Yes, but I don't intend to use it on you." He ignored Sarah's gasp and pointed at Missy. "You're both in a tremendous amount of trouble, and I'm not the trouble that's coming for you."

Darren held up his hands, indicating to his wife and daughter they needed to calm down. "He's here to help us."

"Who are you?" Sarah asked.

"We can chat about that later." Kalen directed Darren to the sliding glass door. "Check to make sure it's unlocked."

Darren questioned Kalen while hurrying to the door. "Unlocked? Shouldn't we lock it?"

"No, we can't lose the element of predictability. He's going to come in through that door."

Sarah moved to her daughter and pulled her close to protect her from Kalen. "I'm sorry, but is someone going to tell us what the hell is going on here?"

"In a matter of minutes, a very bad man is going to come through that door. He's here to kill you all, but mainly, he's here for your daughter."

Sarah and Missy both gasped. Sarah pulled Missy even closer.

Coming Up Short 9

"But I'm here to keep that from happening," Kalen said.

Missy and her mother stood next to a shallow coffee table. On it, two cell phones sat blinking green lights at the top of each. Kalen pointed at them and said to Missy, "Toss those phones on the sofa, please."

"Why?"

"So that you don't decide to call the police. We can't have them involved." Missy reached down, grabbed both devices, and tossed them onto the sofa.

Darren returned from the door. "It's unlocked. It was already unlocked."

This news seemed to unsettle Sarah further. "Oh my God, I could have gotten us killed. I thought I had it locked." She faced Kalen. "How do you know all this?"

"Again, I'll explain later."

She nodded. "So, you'll arrest this man?"

She thinks I'm a cop. Mitchell would love that one.

"Not exactly," Darren said. "You need to run upstairs now and let him take care of…"

Missy extracted herself from her mother. "Oh my God, you're going to kill him, aren't you?"

Coming Up Short 9

Kalen knew his response would forever be etched into the memory of the young girl who stood in a sweatshirt and a pair of shorts. She shook as though the heat had gone off hours before and she would soon die of exposure. Though he wished he didn't have to tell the girl the truth, lying to her would do no good.

He thought of his son, Brent, who wasn't much younger than the girl, and spoke. "The easy thing would be to lie to you, but you're going to be here to see what's going to happen, anyway. The truth is, yes, I'm going to kill him. If I don't, he'll only go on to do what he intends to do here to someone else if he gets away. The best thing that can happen, the only thing, is he dies. The world has enough twisted, demented people like him in it as is." He tried his best to help her see the type of man who was coming after her. "Do you understand?"

With her chin jutted forward, she asked, "What is he here to do to me?"

"Use your imagination," Kalen said flatly.

Missy grabbed her mother by the hand. To Kalen, she said, "Kill him then." Missy pulled her mother forward. "Come on, mom."

Sarah was tugged from the room by her daughter. On her way past Kalen, she said, "Please don't let Darren get hurt."

"I won't," Kalen reassured her.

As they moved out of the room, Kalen said to Darren, "You should go with them."

"No, not an option." He stood his ground at the edge of the living room. "I'm going to be right here to help protect my family."

"Okay." Kalen glanced around.

He won't be of any help, but he has the right to be here.

Behind them, away from the family room, on the other side of the sliding glass door, was the family's kitchen. It held all the normal kitchen appliances. He moved into the room and punched a digital button on the face of the microwave until the light under it switched on. "This, combined with the TV, should give me the light I need." On the counter, next to him, were salt and pepper shakers. They were ceramic molds of an angel (the salt) and the devil (the pepper). He picked up the angel and put it in a pocket.

"What's that for?" Darren asked.

"My intuition says we're going to need it." He said without further explanation. "Go over there and duck down at the end of the sofa."

Darren hustled across the room. Once he reached the place he was to hide, he asked, "What about you?"

Kalen measured the room one last time and picked the space on the far side of the living room's lone chair to hide behind. The spot gave him an excellent firing line toward the kitchen. While he wasn't the outstanding shot that Mitchell was, he had improved his skills with the Beretta greatly. The distance wasn't prohibitive, meaning that he should be able to hit the madman on his way into the house.

Normally, he liked a chance to torture the miserable assholes before ending them, but given the circumstances, he'd settle for a clean shot and one more lunatic gone forever.

Yeah, but what about the bar scene? You had a gut ache. It's yet to come. Will it never happen if you kill him here tonight?

He had no answers to the theoretical questions that ran through his head. Usually, when he had a stomachache with a vision, it meant he was seeing the future. It wasn't like the psychic ability had come with an owner's manual, though. He figured it out as he went along. It was the best he could do.

Kalen withdrew the Beretta and balanced his aim on the arm of the chair. He sighted on the sliding glass door and waited. Hopefully, the silencer Mitchell had given him wouldn't mess with his accuracy too much. While beating the man to death wasn't at all a problem for him, he didn't think Darren could handle it. Shooting him was for the best.

The glass door vibrated as it moved on its track.

Yes, here we go...

Kalen's grip on the pistol relaxed, as he'd been taught to do. He inhaled and let his air out smoothly.

Across from him, Darren whispered a couple of curse words and fell silent.

Coming Up Short 9

"I'm coming for you, Missy." The killer whispered as he pulled the door completely open and entered the room between vertical blind slats. "You rude bitches have this coming." He giggled.

Patience, you need him inside a little more.

The killer placed his second step into the room, allowing the blinds to fall back into place over the open door. Kalen blessed Mitchell for giving him the silencer. Without it, the open door would mean nosey neighbors would call 911 within minutes of the shots.

Kalen sized up the man who had entered the room. He wore the trench coat as anticipated, and it was open down his front. Black boots stuck out the legs of tan slacks. It was all as it had been in most of the visions, with one recent exception. Under the overcoat was a simple black shirt.

Where's the stupid cartoon character T-shirt from earlier? Why'd I see that? It has to have been a future killing that he'll never be able to commit.

Shifting slightly to aim at the dead center of the killer's chest brought a slight creak from the chair Kalen leaned against.

The killer's head snapped around. His eyes locked on Kalen. "What the hell?" He reached inside his coat to withdraw the weapon he intended to use on Missy and Sarah.

Not fast enough, fuck face.

Coming Up Short 9

Kalen squeezed off three very satisfying shots and watched as the silenced muzzle bucked after each. He kept his eyes trained on the chest of the man and watched as little sprays of red erupted from him each time.

The intruder staggered backward before collapsing onto his back on the kitchen floor. The weapon he had drawn from his coat clattered across the kitchen floor tiles.

"Oh, God!" Darren whispered. "Is he dead?"

Kalen stood. "I doubt he can get much more dead."

Moving across the living room with Darren following him, Kalen heard rapid footsteps pounding down a set of stairs.

"Holy shit!" Darren said as he looked down at the dead man. "It's him, that fucker! It's Jimmy!"

"You know him?" Kalen asked as he tucked his weapon away.

"Oh, God!" Sarah and Missy entered the room to wrap their arms around their father. Sarah spoke to her husband, "That's Jimmy from across the road, isn't it?"

"Your damn right it is." Darren ran a hand over his mouth. The surprise on each of their faces wasn't unusual. Regardless of who lay dead on their kitchen floor, shock was anticipated.

Coming Up Short 9

It's finally all real to them. They'll cooperate fully now. They understand how close they were to seeing their family ripped apart.

Kalen withdrew the angel saltshaker and replaced it on the counter next to the devil. He turned and placed a finger on Jimmy's neck to confirm his death. "Yup, dead."

Missy turned away from the dead man. "I think I'm going to be sick."

As their daughter ran for a restroom, Darren asked, "Why'd you take the shaker? You didn't use it."

Kalen shrugged. "I intended to throw it to steer his attention away from us, but he saw us too fast." He pulled the coat sleeve down on Jimmy's left hand to reveal the silly tiger tattoo he remembered from previous visions. "It's him. Hmm."

No clue what that bar scene was all about, but at least these people are safe.

"Yeah, he was going to shoot us, wasn't he?" Darren asked.

"He sure was."

Sarah leveled her gaze at Kalen. "Thank you. Whoever you are, thank you. You saved our lives." A thought came to her and she asked, "This isn't the first time you've done something like this, is it?"

Coming Up Short 9

Missy returned to her mother's side, still shaking, and much paler than before.

"No, he's a killer and he needed to be eliminated." Kalen admitted.

"Who are you, really?" Sarah asked him.

Oh shit, not now...

The light in the room faded from view. Jimmy's dead, twisted, and vacant face floated away in a sea of nothingness. A light fog swirled around him and then parted. A hill formed before him. He stood under moonlight, staring up at a small building on the top of the hill. Its illuminated front filled the night with flashing neon signs, the largest of which stood on the top of the little building.

Gray Horse.

Those two words flicking on and off in neon red floated above a variety of smaller lighted signs. He read words such as Budweiser, Coors, and Hiram Walker and understood what he was seeing. The place was a drinking establishment.

It's a bar.

Kalen read the two flashing words at the top of the building again before it blinked out, along with the moon above. He returned to Darren and Sarah's kitchen.

The Gray Horse. I'm supposed to go there, but why?

Coming Up Short 9

"Are you alright?" Darren asked him.

Kalen realized the three family members all stood staring at him.

"Yeah, I'm good." He assured them.

"Who are you?" Sarah asked again.

Kalen didn't hear her over the rush of thoughts running through his head. "Do you guys know of a bar around town called the Gray Horse? It sits up on a hill…I think." He glanced at Darren.

"Yeah, sure do. It's a few miles away on Route Nine just outside of town." Darren stared at him. "Why?"

"I need you to take me there," Kalen said. The vision could only mean one thing. At the Gray Horse, he'd find another killer.

It could be the guy who likes to spike girls' drinks, but isn't he dead on the floor?

"But what about the…uh, him?" Missy pointed at their dead neighbor on the kitchen floor.

"Don't you worry. I'll be back with someone. His name's Mitchell, and we'll clean everything up." He glanced at the small family, making sure to stare into each of their eyes. "And remember, never a word about any of this. If the cops get involved…"

"Not a word." Darren pledged. "We swear. You saved our lives, we owe you." Darren turned to his wife and daughter. "Throw something like a sheet or blanket over him until he comes back."

"What will you do with him?" Missy asked.

Kalen replied, "You don't want to know." He pivoted away from the kitchen and moved toward the hallway and the front door. "Come on, Darren. We'll need to be fast again."

"Yup." Darren hurried behind him.

Halfway into the hall, Kalen stopped and faced Darren. "And you don't know a Brian?"

"Nope, sure don't," Darren confirmed.

Behind her husband, Sarah spoke up, "Of course you do."

Darren turned to face his wife. "Who?"

She rolled her eyes. "Duh, it's Eddie. I told you this story before. I swear men never listen."

Darren scratched his head and glanced at Kalen while offering him a slight shrug. "Eddie is Eddie. What are you talking about?"

Sarah folded her arms over her chest. "Don't you get sarcastic with me, Darren. We're all stressed, not only you."

Coming Up Short 9

"Of course, I'm sorry, but what are you saying about Eddie?" he asked her again.

"Remember? I told you Eddie goes by Eddie, but that's really his middle name. His real name is Brian." She crumpled her face. "You need to start taking a Ginkgo supplement. Your memory is terrible."

Kalen interrupted the couple to ask a question. "Your nephew, this Brian Eddie, does he happen to own an overcoat like the one that guy's wearing?"

Sarah stared at Kalen. "Yes, he does, as a matter of fact. How'd you know that?" She paused before saying, "Wait a second. I've asked you several times. Who are you?"

The visions were about two different killers all along, not one. Damn, I'm an idiot.

Before turning back toward the front door, Kalen asked her, "Have you ever heard of the killer of killers?"

"Yeah, but he's not real. He's one of those, uh…what do they call them…"

"Urban legends." Missy reminded her.

"That's right," Sarah said. "He's a legend."

Kalen snickered. "Well, sometimes I do feel a little legendary, but don't tell Mitchell I said that. He'll never let me hear the end of it."

Coming Up Short 9

"You?" Sarah asked. "The killer of killers? No, you're not him. If he's real, he's much bigger and tougher than you, for sure." She waved a hand to dismiss the notion.

Geez, I never get any respect, even from the people I save.

Missy stared at Kalen. "You're a looker, though. I'll say that about you."

Sarah tugged her daughter back to her side. "Handsome and much too old for you, young lady." Sarah pointed at Kalen's hand. "And he's married."

"We better go," Kalen told Darren.

As he turned away, Sarah called after him. "We'll see you and Mitchell when you get back and we won't say a word to anyone, but you shouldn't tell your wife about what you did here either, even though you did a good thing. I think it would worry her. And, for God's sake, don't go around telling people you're the killer of killers. It's totally unbelievable."

Rude.

Kalen tossed Darren his car keys. "Let's go."

On the way to the car, Darren said to Kalen, "My wife's right. You shouldn't claim to be something you're not and no one will ever believe you're the killer of killers. I don't know how you knew to come help us, but there's got to be a rational explanation."

Coming Up Short 9

As they climbed into the sedan, Kalen asked, "Why is it so farfetched that I could be him?"

Darren glanced at him as he started the car and backed out of the driveway. "You're too gangly. No, Sarah is right. If the killer of killers is real, he'd be way tougher than you, and you know…much more muscly."

Kalen sighed and stared through the windshield into the night. "Thanks…a lot." He pulled out his phone and sent a text to Mitchell, who undoubtedly was hanging out with Kalen's family playing the role of grandpa.

Hey buddy ol pal! I have some great news! I need you to get off your lazy old ass, tell my wife and son you and I will be home a little later, and then come to the Gray Horse bar. I need some help.

The reply he got was short, which was typical of Mitchell.

There goes a perfectly good evening.

★★★

"You don't want me to stay and help you?" Darren asked from the driver's seat as he pulled up to the side of the Gray Horse bar.

"No, I need you to go back home and hold the fort down until I return. Keep your wife and daughter off their phones and out of the kitchen. Mitchell and I will be along shortly."

Coming Up Short 9

Darren asked him, "This Mitchell, who is he?"

"Just about the best guy you'd ever meet. He's also an old curmudgeon and grump." Kalen opened his door and paused. "Don't tell him I said any of those things, please. And remind your wife and daughter…" Kalen held a finger to his lips before departing the car.

★★★

She was about as stupid a woman as he and Ace had ever encountered. Typically arrogant, and full of herself, but at least she was non-combative. Of course, he hadn't let Ace take the lead on this one. As he pretended to listen to her rattle on endlessly about her life and the wants and desires she had that could only be filled by the right man, he glanced at his friend.

Though the idiot blonde was unaware, Ace sat across from them in a booth. He was simply waiting for him to coerce the woman from the bar.

It would be easy to do this time. He only needed her to leave the table for a moment. He had something extra special to put in her mixed drink. It would make her much easier to manipulate and make it easy for him and Ace to have their fun.

★★★

The inside of the bar was the same dark place from his vision. The number of neon beer signs inside the place was only rivaled by those on the exterior of the building. It was the type of place Kalen had spent far too much time in his college days before meeting Tish (for the second time). It had been a time of feeling sorry for himself that he had let the woman of his dreams get away from him once upon a time (also Tish).

Loud music pounded through the small bar. It was a mix of country and old rock, played far too loudly. The dance floor was only partially filled with people moving with the swaying motions of their intentions. The women on the floor were doing their best to show their men how sexy they were, and their men were doing their best to tell them they already knew.

Kalen spied the blonde woman in the short black dress and the overcoat-wearing man where he expected them to be and sat down at an empty table. His vantage point was from behind the man (whose name was probably Brian) and facing the woman. His view was from the same perspective as in his vision.

The booths around the bar filled, for the most part, with couples who were hanging out with other couples. Across from the coated man was a man by himself. He wore a leather jacket and seemed to keep an eye on the man in the coat.

I should tell him he's in the wrong bar.

"Can I get you something to drink, Mr. good-looking?"

Kalen glanced up to stare into the eyes of a brunette server who smiled back at him. "No, thank you. I won't be here long."

She leaned closer to speak over the music without shouting. "What if I offered you something off the menu...so to speak?" Her breath tickled his ear.

Coming Up Short 9

Holding up his left hand, Kalen answered, "I'm flattered, and also very much in love with my amazing wife."

The girl stuck out her lower lip in a feigned pout. "All the good ones are taken."

He smiled at her. "You don't know if I'm good. For all you know, I could be some kind of badass killer out stalking other killers, trying to make the world a safer place."

She placed a hand over her mouth to cover her laughter. "You're cute."

Kalen frowned. "You don't think I look like a tough, badass dude?"

"You're cute and definitely funny, but no." Her hand fell away from her mouth. She winked at him and turned to move on to another table. "If you change your mind, let me know...and I'm not talking about a beer."

I need to hit the gym...or grow a beard or something.

Kalen diverted his attention back to the man in the overcoat and watched as the blonde woman slipped from her barstool. Brian reached out a hand and steadied her as she staggered.

She's heading to the restroom. He'll try to put that shit in her drink in a second.

Coming Up Short 9

Kalen slid out of his seat and approached the man, Brian, from behind. The blonde hurried to the restroom and already, Brian had the small glass vial in his hand.

Standing at the backside of the table, Kalen placed his hand over the rim of the blonde woman's drink.

As Brian unscrewed the lid and reached for the drink, he bumped into Kalen's hand. He turned on his seat and stared into Kalen's eyes. "Excuse me. That's my lady's drink. What are you doing?"

Kalen leaned closer and shouted, "I'm keeping you from spiking her drink." He nodded at the clear vial in Brian's hand.

He wants to lie and deny what I'm saying, but the evidence is in his hand.

Before Brian could speak, Kalen said, "Nice T-shirt. Did you pick that up at Baby Gap?" The way the shirt folded inside the coat, it appeared Foghorn had been beheaded.

"Hey, dude. It won't be that hard for me to stand up and kick your ass. Get the fuck out of here!"

Kalen noted the man in the leather jacket had slipped to the edge of his seat in the booth across from them. He stared at their interaction with an angry curiosity.

Could be just another drunk dude looking to join a fight, and he could be more than that.

Coming Up Short 9

Kalen pulled the woman's drink toward him. "You see, if I did that, you'd dump that poison in her drink, and then later on, she'd end up raped and dead. Isn't that right, Eddie?"

At the mention of his middle name, Brian's face flushed, and his face paled in the neon atmosphere. "How the hell do you know my name?"

Kalen sighed. "Well, I mean, it's not really your name, is it now, Brian?"

Brian stood from his stool. "Hey now, what the fuck? You been spying on me?"

"Eddie? What's going on?" The blonde had arrived back at the table.

Kalen offered his hand to her. "Hi there. Today's your lucky day. You see, your date, Eddie here, whose real name is Brian, was getting ready to spike your drink." Kalen pointed down at Brian's hand. "See that vial? Yeah, turns out he's a rapist and I think he might also be a killer, although, to be fair, he and I haven't gotten that far in our conversation yet."

Her eyes, ablaze with a sudden fury, flashed to Brian. "You piece of shit!" She spun on wobbly legs and stormed toward the bar exit.

"You son of a bitch!" Brian tucked the small glass bottle back into his pocket and shoved Kalen in the chest. Foghorn had regained his body as Brian's jacket pulled back at the sides. The cartoon bird seemed to mock Kalen as he slipped in a spilled drink. Losing his balance, Kalen's left foot caught the blonde's stool, and he fell to the floor.

"Whoa, Buddy! You alright?" A man in jeans, cowboy boots, and a red and black plaid shirt stepped close to Kalen.

Kalen tried to get to his feet and slipped again. "Dammit!"

The cowboy clutched Kalen by the arm and pulled him to his feet. He pointed at Kalen's shoes. "That's why no one wears sneakers in here man, the floor's always a mess with spilled beer."

Kalen glanced around the room. Brian was gone. "Did you see where the man who hit me went?"

"Now, take my word for it. It ain't worth it. Let it go and let me buy you a drink." He offered his hand. "Name's Steven."

Kalen shook his hand and said, "Thank you, Steven, and I might take you up on that one day, but right now, I need to find that guy. He's going to hurt the woman he's with very badly if I don't."

"Oh!" Steven released his hand and pointed toward the exit. "Well, shoot! He followed her outside."

★★★

He didn't know whether he wanted to wait outside for the dumbass who had ruined his plan or chase after the woman. As he ran out of the bar and into the night, he realized the woman hadn't gotten as far away as he thought she would. She was only ten yards away to his right, stumbling toward the parking lot. He also understood there was no one else around.

Thoughts of waiting to kill the asshole from the bar exited his head. The thirst he always felt when on the cusp of choking the life out of yet another whore peaked inside him. Both time and opportunity still existed to accomplish what he wanted. Hopefully, Ace would leave the bar and find him, or at least take care of the little prick who decided playing hero was a good idea.

Brian chased after Susan (if that was her real name) and caught her on his eighth step.

"Leave me a..." She started to scream but was cut off when he slugged her on the side of her head.

Dazed, she staggered into him, making it easy to slip an arm around her waist and yank her backward and around the side of the bar.

On his way into the shadows, he checked the front of the bar again. Still, no one was outside.

Ace would miss out on all the fun this time. Hopefully, he would at least find a way to eliminate the bastard inside the bar. The dude had a wild look in his eyes that was more than a little unsettling.

★★★

Coming Up Short 9

The ground outside the bar had an early layer of fog floating over it. With each of his steps, it stirred and swirled, unhappy with his intrusion.

Kalen stared out at the parking lot, with its one lonely lamppost, and scanned for a sign of the blonde woman or the dipshit named Brian. The place was void of humanity, and it seemed he had stepped into a nightmare dystopian scene in a horror novel. Other than a lone pair of headlights at the base of the hill below the bar, he was alone.

"Shit, where'd they go?"

To his left, the driveway from the base of the hill reached the parking lot. That side of the building was extremely exposed.

If he got his hands on her, he didn't take her there. Too much risk.

Kalen turned to his right and hurried to the far side of the Gray Horse.

He rounded the corner and slid to a stop. Ahead of him, a single light hung from the roof of the building. Standing under the lamp was Brian, his overcoat twisting as he struggled to wrap his hands around the throat of the blonde woman. He had her up against the side of the bar, her feet rising off the ground.

Kalen hurried toward them, running, but trying to make his steps soft on the hard ground. The element of surprise was his dearest friend until he could reach Brian.

Coming Up Short 9

★★★

The cockiness of an attractive woman, who was accustomed to men falling all over themselves to speak to her, had vanished from her face fast. She was his now, and the stare in her eyes told him so. Soon, he'd have her on the ground, and when he did, he'd have his way with her before completely choking the life from her attractive body.

"You're what's wrong with this world!" He seethed at her. "You think because you're good-looking that you can do whatever you want, and treat people however you wish, but who's in control now, bitch?"

He leaned forward to lick her face when the air in his lungs was punched out. Something hammered him in the back, causing him to stumble forward. At the feel of a sharp pain in his back, he released the woman and reached behind him. The woman slid from him, down the wall, to the ground. She lay on her side, coughing, desperately pulling air into her lungs.

Who had found him? There was no way Ace had turned on him, no way.

Before he could pivot to face his attacker, another blow landed against his ribs and the pain was enough to drive him to his knees.

He landed with a thud on the ground next to the woman. Her eyes were open wide and filled with terror. She stared up beyond him and over his shoulder at his enemy.

Coming Up Short 9

An arm snaked around his throat, and he was dragged across the ground and thrown into a shadow, out of the range of the small lamp on the outside of the building.

"Who the fuck are you?" He asked the towering figure who stood over him. His question was answered with a kick to his head and the little light in the night blinked out.

★★★

Kalen helped the woman to her feet. She allowed him to help her, though he could see the fear in her eyes.

"You're okay. I'm here to help you. I hurt him to protect you." He reassured her as she regained her feet.

"You're the guy from inside the bar…" She stared at him, unsure about him still.

"Yes, I am."

She coughed and wiped a strand of phlegm from her mouth. "Gross, sorry."

"Don't worry about it."

She stood, shaky, but facing him. "Brian was going to kill me."

"Yeah, he sure was."

Coming Up Short 9

"And somehow, you knew that didn't you?" She asked. Her hair hung around her head in damp strands. The exertion of fighting against Brian had taken its toll.

"I did." Kalen stuffed his hands in his pockets, so she understood he was no threat. "And now you have an important decision to make."

"About?" She seemed weary, and he didn't blame her.

He pointed at Brian, who lay in a heap. Only his boots protruded from the shadow of a large tree. He would be out for at least another few minutes. "If we call the police, they'll arrest him, but since you didn't die, he'll get bonded out soon enough and he'll be free to run around, raping and killing, until they catch him again. He'll definitely attack other women because this isn't the first time he's done this. Unfortunately, the cops won't be able to prove that, at least not before he can get out. He might even come after you again."

The last thing he told her caused a shiver to go up her spine. He watched her shudder and glance at the man in the shadows. She asked, "What else can we do?"

"You can walk away, pretend it never happened, and I'll take care of it." He stared her in the eyes and added, "If I take care of him, no one will ever see him again."

She glanced from Kalen back to the man on the ground. "I don't want that on my conscience, but I also don't want him to hurt others, or me, again." She dusted the dirt from the sleeve on her right arm and spoke softly. "So, I don't want to make the decision. I'm going to leave it up to you, but I assume if I walk out of here, there will be no chance I'll ever see him again."

"That's right."

She nodded. "Okay, deal. Thank you for saving me."

Kalen felt the old anger in him rise and only what was about to happen to Brian could put out those fires. The poor woman would suffer PTSD for years because of the past few moments. She was truly lucky to be alive and wouldn't appreciate that for a long time. "You're welcome."

"I know who you are." She said. "You have to be him."

"Who's that?"

She moved next to him, no longer afraid. "You're the guy from those news stories. You're the killer of killers, aren't you?"

Kalen smiled despite his vitriol. "And if I am?"

She returned his grin. "I'd only say thank you some more."

"Again, you're welcome."

As she stepped away, she said, "You're as good-looking and tough as I imagined. You're exactly what I thought you'd be like, and you're a gentleman. I saw your wedding ring, so I'll leave it at that."

Coming Up Short 9

Well, take that, Darren, Sarah, and others. It's about damn time someone thought I fit the billing.

★★★

Brian came to, with Kalen leaning over him. He stared up into Kalen's face. "Who the hell are you?" Dirt streaks lined his face. His dark hair had leaves matted in it. To Kalen, he appeared to be a homeless man who woke up after sleeping off a metric shit ton of drinking.

Kalen held the Beretta in his right hand. The muzzle was pointed at Brian's heart. Foghorn Leghorn didn't seem amused with him at all. Maybe it was the silencer that angered the fictitious bird.

I say, I say, boy…I'm going to let God fix it. If I fix it, I'm going to jail – Ha!

"I've covered this a couple of times tonight, but no one wants to believe me. I'll just say I'm the guy who's made a practice of killing piles of crap like you."

Brian twitched, his face giving away the fear that washed through his head. "That guy is made up."

Kalen yawned. "Yeah, that's what everyone thinks, but…wrong. Here I am, the killer of killers." He wanted to bow, but wouldn't give Brian a chance to attack.

"I thought you'd be more…"

Coming Up Short 9

Kalen interrupted him. "If you say tough, it's seriously going to piss me off, even more than I am already."

Brian tried to sit up but a kick in his chest sent him back to the soil. He glared at Kalen and asked, "And what makes you so much better than me? If you're who you say you are, you do the same things as me. Killing is killing, and something tells me you're as addicted to it as I am."

Kalen smirked at the thought that he and Brian had anything in common. "I'm nothing like you. You kill the innocent. You destroy families and ruin lives. I, on the other hand, improve society by eliminating people like you."

"How'd you find me?"

Kalen shrugged, "Eh, you wouldn't believe me if I told you."

"Try me." Brian pressed.

Kalen placed a small amount of pressure on the Beretta's trigger. "I saw the depraved, shitty things you did to many women, right here in my head. I watched the torture you brought to innocent lives, and I hated you for every single bit of it."

"Those bitches all had it coming."

Kalen sighed. "And that right there is why you have to die."

Coming Up Short 9

"Wait!"

Kalen pulled the trigger twice and watched Brian jerk in response. The shot that killed Brian had also murdered the bird on his shirt. Foghorn had a new hole in his head. Kalen stared down into empty, fading eyes, and grinned. "I'd do that a million times a day, all day, every day if I could." The satisfaction of watching a murderer like Brian die always brought him happiness.

He pushed the dead man further into the shadows and then retrieved his phone from a pocket.

A text from Mitchell had been waiting for him.

I'm here. Where are you?

Kalen typed:

Outside on the…

His fingers fell away from the keyboard at the feel of cold metal pressed into his neck. One hand grabbed him by the shoulder, the other reached around his neck to place a knife against his throat.

Kalen poked the phone back into his pocket and stared at the ground near his feet. Limited light cast to him from the lone light on the side of the bar shined on the ground around him. "Ace, I presume."

"How do you know my name?" A gruff voice spoke into his ear.

… Coming Up Short 9

The breath that hit his nostrils smelled like beer and pickles. "Well, now I know what you had for a snack in there. Thanks for that. It's a shame I'm too late to give you some solid advice."

"You're too late because I'm going to kill you for what you done to Brian." Ace's voice reflected the anger he felt as he stared into the shadows at his dead partner.

Kalen snickered, and the knife pressed in harder on him. He said, "What I was going to say is, the next time you go raping and murdering innocent women who want nothing to do with you, you might at least consider a breath mint. Yikes, the combination of fried pickles and beer does not exactly say please trust me, so I can take you outside and kill you."

Ace laughed. "Oh, you're one of those smartass types. I just told you I'm going to kill you, and you want to play the part of the tough guy, huh?"

On the ground, to Kalen's left, a shadow grew from behind them. It was what he'd been watching and waiting for. "Well, duh, because when I said I was too late to give you that good advice, I meant to say that it was because you'd never get a chance to kill again."

"You know, I've about had enough of your fucking stupid mouth."

Kalen replied, "That's good because you're out of time."

"Huh?"

Coming Up Short 9

"Mitchell, you can kill him now. He's boring me."

Kalen felt the man behind him jerk. Kalen shoved the knife away from his throat as the man slid to the ground. Turning around, Kalen watched as Mitchell bent over and wiped a large knife blade on Ace's leather jacket. Kalen complained, "Geez, wait until the last possible moment why don't you?"

Mitchell, his long-standing friend and partner, stood and smiled. "You wanted your little dramatic moment, so I gave it to you."

Mitchell was an older man, who despite his years was still sharp as a tack and a very effective FBI profiler. He was also a man of morals who, like Kalen, had tired of watching the worst of humanity make bail, only to go back out into the world and kill innocent people. Kalen loved him like family, and he knew the old man felt the same way about him, although he'd never admit it. "Yes, okay, true. So, what should we do with these fuckers?"

Mitchell shrugged and tucked his knife back inside a jacket pocket. "That's your deal. See you at the car." He started to turn away from Kalen.

"You'll back the car up here so we can load them up and go get the other one?"

"Yeah, alright. Sure." He said as he walked to the parking lot. "Be right back."

★★★

Coming Up Short 9

The two dead men were rolled in plastic and stuffed into the trunk of the FBI-issued sedan. Kalen wiped the sweat from his forehead and said, "Should we head over to Darren and Sarah's house now?" Fortunately, so far, no one had exited the bar and noticed them parked around the corner.

Mitchell used a hand towel to clean himself. "Nah, I'm all about helping those in need, but this is over the top."

"You mean a nice guy like me can't catch a ride to the next crime scene?" Kalen grinned. He loved the back-and-forth banter he'd developed over time with the older man.

"A nice guy, yes. You…eh…I'm lukewarm on the idea."

Kalen sighed, although he had a hard time hiding the grin plastered on his face. "Okay, well, I didn't want to go here, but you are living in my house and eating my food these days."

"Ha! Your food? It's Tish's food, and she makes it for me. Tonight, she made my favorite lasagna, and you had to come along and interrupt my enjoyment of it. Without you, I'd be snoozing in front of the TV now with a belly full." Mitchell pulled a set of car keys from his pocket. "I still don't know how you talked that lovely woman into marrying you. She could have done much better."

Kalen moved to the passenger door and opened it. "Sadly, I agree with you. For the longest time, I questioned if maybe Tish has vision problems." He plopped into the front seat as Mitchell climbed into the driver's seat.

Mitchell said, "You know how some people are color blind?"

"Yeah?"

The old man continued, "Tish must be - pain in the ass - blind."

"Ahh, I don't believe you. I know you love me."

Mitchell forced his smile away. "Don't get too carried away or you'll end up walking." He started the car and pulled away from the Gray Horse. "So, this family you saved. Do they know to keep their mouths shut?"

"Yeah, and they will. They know I saved them. They're grateful." Kalen said. "At least someone appreciates me. Either way, we should stick to the shadows for a while, probably. Or at least I should."

Mitchell nodded his agreement. "Right, be like Croatoan for a while."

"Croatoan?" Kalen had heard the word before, but he couldn't recall it.

"Within the Fog? Welch horror novel? Ring any bells?" Mitchell asked.

"No, not at all."

Coming Up Short 9

"Eh, you're not a reader. It's over your head. You're missing out, but I won't waste my time telling you about it."

Kalen pondered the name and the book. "Welch, the writer who lives over in Greeley?"

"Yeah, that's him."

Kalen smirked. "Nah, I don't like him. My secret life has enough horror in it. I don't know how you can read that stuff."

Mitchell waved him off. "Leave it to you to miss out on the good stuff. Even Tish likes him, but you do you."

"No choice about it. All I know is how to be me."

"Yay for the rest of us," Mitchell groused.

Coming Up Short 9

The end!

Exclusive First Reader Membership

Did you know that various books in the **Coming Up Short** universe have hit #1 on the Amazon charts multiple times?

True story!

And that is all thanks to you, dearest loyal reader!

The loyal following of this series, often compared to The Twilight Zone, Night Shift, Scary Stories to Tell in the Dark and other anthologies has prompted Charles Welch to sign off on a one-time, exclusive opportunity.

Want an opportunity to own the forthcoming Hardback **Coming Up Short Special Edition - Author's Selection**?

What is the **Coming Up Short Special Edition – Author's Selection**?

Soon, Charles Welch will release a Hardcover illustrated book featuring his favorite stories from the 9 volumes of **Coming Up Short**, as well as 4 new stories that will not be released anywhere else, **EVER!** AND – the volume will feature a color illustration of his favorite scene from each story!

This rare book will not be released on Amazon or any other retail outlet.

Coming Up Short 9

In addition, Charles will offer an even rarer version of this book, **The Midnight Edition**, that will feature 5 new stories and black and white illustrations from each tale!

So, how do you get a signed copy of these books and other collectible **Coming Up Short** merchandise?

Join our exclusive Reader's Club for updates on when these works will be available, how you can order your copy, as well as other information on upcoming releases.

Exclusive First Reader Membership

https://mailchi.mp/a60a000b28db/exclusive-first-reader-membership

Coming Up Short 1, 2, 3, 4, 5, 6, 7 & 8

Coming Up Short 9

Available on Amazon!

Please enjoy the first few chapters of my novel – Laughers!

Laughers

BOOK 1

THE BEGINNING OF THE STORM

ONE

Every time Candy Reynolds wondered why she had taken a job with so much travel, she remembered what it felt like not to know where her and her son's next meal would come from. The constant, nagging phone calls because the maxed-out credit cards were past due and the late notices on her apartment door regarding rent were still stressful. Even after months of working and paying her way out of debt, she could remember the sick feeling of failure.

Financially, things had improved since accepting

her position as a traveling medical sales representative. The unfortunate cost of the travel was a drastic sacrifice of time with her son, who would soon graduate from high school. Matt was a great kid and had never given her an ounce of trouble, at least nothing compared to the trouble she had caused them both when he had been a little boy.

She placed her suitcase in the trunk of her aging Honda Civic at the Colorado Springs airport, tossed her handbag onto the front passenger seat, and started the car. It wasn't much to look at with its fading silver paint and the dent in the front driver's fender (courtesy of an ex-boyfriend) but the vehicle was reliable. It still delivered, and she needed it to stay that way for a while.

After driving to the airport exit, Candy inserted her parking stub into the parking kiosk. The lights in front of her flashed green and the bar guarding the exit from the parking lot raised. She sighed and began the trip home. The skies that had been gray upon landing at the airport were now dark and heavy. She had lived in Colorado Springs her entire life. When heavy, dark clouds came over the Rocky Mountains in winter, and they hung up above the city, the metro area got snow,

Coming Up Short 9

heavy snow. The forecast was for at least eighteen inches, and Candy thought the angry skies would deliver much more.

Academy Boulevard was packed with the usual late afternoon, early evening traffic. The drive home would take time. The slow going was a temporary sacrifice to get to the much smaller, more remote roads that she typically used to go home from the airport. Living in the southwest part of town had its advantages, even though it was not the nicest area in the Springs. One of those advantages was the view of Pike's Peak and the mountain range that towered over the city. Another bonus was that she could usually avoid most of the congestion, once she cleared Academy.

She drove, progressively gaining speed, watching the snowflakes fall while avoiding the view of the row of bars on her right. She could not look at them since she had found sobriety. It had been years since she had taken a drink, but it felt like yesterday that the line of drinking establishments had been her home away from home.

Candy focused her gaze on the road in front of her as traffic began moving again, feeling a little nudge of shame. Her stomach tightened as she thought of all she had put Matt through with her drinking. She was lucky that she still had him, and yet, despite the horror show her drinking had created at one point in their lives, the part of her that craved the warm buzz of a Jack Daniels high still yearned. It still called to her, pleading for one drink. One little sip, no more. She imagined a little devil in her mind, his empty drinking glass extended, begging. Only, it wouldn't be one little drink or one little sip. It would be one drink that led to another and another until she fell off her barstool and ended the night by staggering home with someone she didn't know. The little devil knew that's how it would go despite his promises of just one drink, because that little devil, the alcoholic in her, was also an accomplished liar.

The falling snowflakes were increasing in size. She forced her thoughts away from her past. She had years of sobriety under her belt, and she clung to them. They were always out in front of her, thoughts waving like the banner at a newly opened business. Each accumulated day, week, month, and year of sobriety lent validity to her new life, to her investment in her son and the future. Matt was proud of her, and that mattered more than any drink or buzz ever would. She had even noticed in the past year that he had stopped checking for stashed bottles in the apartment. For a long time, he had hovered near her when she came home to see if he could detect the aroma of hard alcohol.

He was unaware that she knew he did those things. She had never found it annoying. More than anything, it had been a constant reminder to her of the importance of her sobriety. To have made her son proud of her for so long mattered the most to her. It was even more important than their recent financial success, although they weren't yet out of the woods when it came to money.

Candy reminded herself of her one day at a time philosophy. It was like recovering from any illness or injury, not every day would be spectacular. If healing were a line, it would not be straight, but a climbing line that dipped and jumped back up in fits and starts. As long as that line kept rising over time, though, she was on the right track. That was what had been happening since she had ditched the bottle - gradual improvement, which was good enough for her. They were getting there, and she had become a good parent. Her relationship with her son was much better than when she had been a shithead,

Coming Up Short 9

drunken monster of an absent mother.

She turned the economy car off the busy boulevard and onto a smaller two-lane road and headed west. The intensity of the falling flakes was already gaining momentum. People were driving much slower on the back-road than they had been on the boulevard.

Matt was on her mind. She had been thinking about him throughout her recent trip. He had bought his girlfriend a promise ring and intended to give it to her later in the evening. Candy liked Kyra a lot. She and Matt, despite their youth and inexperience, had a genuine relationship. It was one to be envied, as she had never found one like it.

She was also concerned because her son wanted to give Kyra the ring before she went away to college. Long-distance relationships gave her the shudders. She had tried holding a relationship with a man who had lived in Kansas at one point and had only found failure. In fairness, Matt and Kyra were a much stronger couple than she and Stan had been.

Who knew? It could be fine, but Kyra Waters

came from a family in which money reigned supreme. Her father made a mint, and her mother spent a mint. Kyra seemed to have different values than her parents, and Candy hoped it stayed that way. She had met the fabulous Ron and Kathy Waters a couple of times and had been judged by them. Their determination being that she was below them, because of her financial circumstances. They also had passed judgment on her son, even though they didn't say it in so many words. Matt was very aware that they did not want him and Kyra together long-term. Kathy had even referred to Kyra's involvement with Matt as a 'phase'.

Candy made a right turn and jumped onto an even smaller road. The Honda slid a bit in the accumulating snow. For a moment she considered backtracking and taking a much longer route. Her desire to be home for her son pushed her forward. It was important to be there for him to either celebrate his success or console him if it didn't go well.

Kyra was headed to sunny Southern California for college. Matt would stay in town to get his general education requirements accomplished at the local community college. If Kyra turned Matt down, it would be over the distance between Colorado and California.

She took a deep breath and uttered a quick prayer that all would go well for her son. The nerves she felt were as strong, as if she were the one giving someone a ring representing long-term commitment.

As she drove, she reached across the front cabin of the car and dug in her purse for her phone. A quick call to Matt, wishing him good luck wouldn't hurt anything. She could already hear him playing it cool, even though she knew he was a nervous wreck.

It'll be fine, mom. Me and Kyra are good. Don't worry.

She plucked the phone from the bag and clicked the power button.

She diverted her eyes from the road for a moment to dial and found a blank screen. Pressing the power button again did not help.

"Dead. It's dead."

She tossed it back into her bag. The phone had

been low on power before leaving Chicago. It had been her plan to charge it at the airport, and she had forgotten. Running late to the airport had its consequences, and a phone with no battery was hers.

A gust of wind hit the side of the car. It slipped for a moment and then regained traction. A surge of adrenaline caused her to press the brake harder than she needed to, and the small Honda skidded again. One of the budgetary items she had been putting off was a needed set of new tires. She had hoped that she could get through another winter without spending the five hundred dollars it would cost. As the snow piled up in front of her, she regretted the choice to put the expenditure off. New tires would be a tremendous help in the storm.

She slowed the pace of the vehicle to twenty miles an hour. So far, other than the flashing lights of a police cruiser ahead on the side of the road, hers was the only car she had seen.

She approached the police car. Its lights strobed the falling snow in what seemed like a warning against driving further up the road. So far, her windshield wipers had done an admirable job of keeping up with the weather. Through the back-and-forth motion of the wiper blades, she could see a short police officer and another, a taller man standing beside the cruiser. Neither of them wore jackets or coats. They did not seem to notice the extreme weather.

Candy dropped the Honda to five miles an hour and crawled past the two men in the oncoming lane. She stared out the passenger side of her car as she drew even with them. Something was off. She couldn't put a finger on what it was, but the cop seemed relaxed with the man in front of him, a little too relaxed.

She craned her neck to see through the frost on the car's side window. As she moved past the two men, they both looked at her inside the car and waved.

It wasn't a friendly 'Hey how are you doing?' type of wave. The two were laughing as they each flapped an open hand in her direction. The cop was laughing so hard that the gun on his belt bounced up and down. His gesture was an exaggeration of a neighborly hello. The two of them extended their arms and made windmilling circular motions after waving at her, which only caused them to laugh even harder.

Candy had the Honda far enough past the police cruiser and the man's SUV that she had to switch her eyes to her rearview mirror. She could see the cop poke the man in the chest and then bend over, slapping at his knee as he continued his hysterics.

The man in front of him tilted his head back, howling with hilarity. He lowered his head and balled up a fist. His arm reared back as a wind gust covered the back of her car with snow. She could no longer see either of the vehicles or the lights of the cruiser. The sun was dipping behind the mountain peaks, making visibility more difficult.

"What the hell was that all about?"

It had looked as though the man was going to punch the cop, but they had both been laughing. It made no sense.

Chunks of snow hit the undercarriage of her car. The loud noise drew her gaze back to the road in front of her. She had drifted onto the wrong side of the road.

Coming Up Short 9

"You're damn lucky no one was coming."

She righted her course on the road, pulling the vehicle back into her lane. For the first time, a worried feeling began gnawing at her gut. She should have stayed on the main roads. The snow had come on much faster than she had expected, and much faster than was typical. She already had the heater in the compact car cranked as far as it would go, and yet she still froze. Not having a working phone made her anxiety climb even higher.

"What kind of idiot drives through a blizzard on back roads without a working phone?" She paused, realizing that she was trying to comfort herself with the sound of her voice. "Me, that's who."

An attempt at increasing her speed only resulted in the car sliding toward the shoulder.

"Shit!"

She righted the car and slowed again. At her current rate of speed, it would be hours before she could get back to her apartment. It was becoming difficult to see the road because there were no tracks from other vehicles to follow. When she had first turned onto it, there had been only a slight accumulation. As she pushed ahead, she guessed the storm had already dumped six inches in the area. If the accumulation didn't slow down, she would eventually get stuck.

She saw a familiar large tree ahead. Its branches swayed in the winter wind. Snow plastered against its west-facing side. She knew the road curved away from the tree to the south and then bent back to the north on its westward course. Leaning forward over the steering wheel, she squinted into the blizzard. She could not see where the road curved away. Everything was covered in a layer of white.

She anticipated the upcoming turn and steered the car to her left. She wanted to stop and check the road, but knew that stopping the car could mean she would not get it moving again.

"Dammit."

She pulled a little further to her left and felt the sway of uncontrolled motion. The car slid toward the opposite side of the road. She tried to increase her speed. The tires only spun in place while the car slid sideways.

Coming Up Short 9

She pushed on the brake and turned the steering wheel in the skid's direction.

The car stopped moving, facing the wrong direction, in the wrong lane. Candy pushed the gas pedal. The car slipped further. She tried to reverse. It moved a few inches backward before the tires spun. She put the Honda back in drive and rocked the car forward. It moved half of what it had, moved backward and stalled. She continued to try rocking the Honda back and forth, hoping it would gain traction.

"Shit, shit, SHIT!" Candy slammed her fist against the steering wheel after several failed attempts. She turned on the hazard lights and grabbed her bag from the front seat. She tossed open her door and stepped into the cold. Snow blasted against her face. She zipped the top of her coat as far as it would go and shoved the car door shut. Looking to the west, she searched her memory for what was ahead on the empty road.

There had been an old farmhouse to the south. She was sure of it. It was the type of old-style house she had always imagined owning. She admired the home each time she had used the road to come home from a road trip. It was up ahead, to her left, not far off the road.

Placing one unsteady foot in front of the other, she began her trek to the house or the first sign of humanity that she could find. She needed a phone to get a hold of Matt. He could help her find a tow company, if they were even still operating.

Tears threatened to fall. She clamped her jaw shut tight and began stomping forward into the pending darkness and the raging conditions. Her resolution was to not let her emotions get the better of her.

TWO

At one point, while high stepping across a drift of snow, Candy tripped and fell onto her knees. Snow covered her to mid-thigh. Her face had come free of the top of her coat and the wind stung her skin with ice bullets. She was grateful that she had remembered her gloves and hat for her trip to the windy city. She was especially appreciative of them after falling into the drift.

Coming Up Short 9

Climbing free of the heavy pile of snow, she slipped and tumbled down an embankment, landing on her side. Wet snow had gotten shoved up her nose. Candy snorted and blew her nose, a stream of water and snot blasting into the wind. She regained her feet and found herself staring through a cluster of trees. The roofline of a building was visible through their limbs.

Plunging ahead, her hopes rising; she stared at the front porch of the farmhouse. It was the one she remembered. Moonlight illuminated it more than any remaining sunlight. The sun was finally on the cusp of heading to the other side of the world, where it would share its warmth with Earth's other peoples.

Finding the two-story home with its covered front porch and unmistakable light blue color seemed like the completion of a last-second hail Mary pass. She was catching her touchdown as the clock expired and her team was down seven points. She would still need to kick the extra point to stay alive for overtime. That meant someone needed to be home to open the door.

She limped to the house, taking giant, exaggerated steps to clear the drifts of snow in her path.

Coming Up Short 9

After climbing the few steps to the front porch, she was exhausted but exhilarated. She had not allowed herself to contemplate what would happen if she didn't find the house. Now that she had found it, she could put off thoughts of dying in a snowdrift.

The little devil who had been her constant companion during her drinking days cleared his throat and told her that if she was going to die, frozen and lost in the snow, that it would be a better departure if their good friend Jack Daniels was along for the ride. She hushed the little demon and knocked on the front door of the house, seeing no obvious doorbell.

No one opened the door, so she beat on it harder. When the door had still not opened, she cupped her hands to an adjacent window, looking for signs of movement inside of the home. She could see through the white lace curtains. A small, formal living room sat empty. A fire burned in a fireplace at the back of the room. Her mouth hung open at the sight of the small fire. Her skin prickled, and chills ran up her back. She imagined lounging in front of the fire on the plush-looking sofa that sat in the center of the room.

Coming Up Short 9

She returned to the closed door and knocked again, longer than the first two times combined. She hit it loud enough that she was sure the dead would rise from their graves to find her as the source of their disturbance.

She waited, blowing warm air into her gloved hands. It had been at least another minute, with no response. Candy decided that it couldn't hurt to at least try the door handle. She wasn't one to break into a stranger's home, but if she couldn't warm up, she would die. She did not feel like a drama queen for thinking she could die in the elements. The news was filled with people who had died in such conditions during Colorado's winters. It was not her desire to become a fatality statistic, and she could use a phone to call Matt.

Grabbing the door handle, she twisted the knob. She was surprised when it turned in her grip. She hesitated and returned to the living room window to peer inside. The burning fire told her someone had to be home. Maybe they couldn't hear her knocking on the door over the gusting wind.

Frozen pellets stung the side of her face as she

contemplated the whereabouts of the homeowner. She reasoned it couldn't hurt to at least open the door and call out to see if she could get someone's attention.

Candy grabbed the door handle again and looked around the porch, feeling as though she were a criminal. What would happen to her if the person who lived in the remote home was watching her from somewhere on the property? They could sneak up on her and attack her with no warning at all. They could also be waiting inside to shoot her for breaking into their home. She lectured herself for her paranoia and turned the door handle. It opened.

She could smell cooking food the moment she pushed her head inside the warmth of the home. Her stomach rumbled. The aroma was all she could think about, her frozen appendages forgotten.

"Hello?" she called out to the home's interior. "Is anyone home?"

The home was silent.

"Can anyone hear me? My name is Candy. I hate to disturb you, but I could use a little help." She stepped inside the house and closed the front door behind her. The scents of cooking meat grew much stronger.

She stepped further into the small living room. It had been since a small breakfast sandwich at O'Hare airport that she had last eaten.

Candy mumbled to herself, "Oh, God, I'm so hungry."

The warmth of the fire was already thawing her chilled muscles and joints. She removed the cap from her head and ran a hand through her long black hair. It was as wet as if she had stepped from the shower.

"Hello, I'm sorry I barged into your home, but I'm freezing. My car got stuck on the highway and I need to use a phone. Is anyone here?" Candy stepped further into the room. For the first time she was aware of a door in the back corner, opposite of the fireplace. She moved to the front of the fire and held her gloved hands before her to heat them. While drying the water out of her hair and clothes, she noticed an old-fashioned, corded phone sitting on a table next to the fireplace.

Coming Up Short 9

"Oh, thank God."

Candy removed her gloves and grabbed up the phone from its cradle. She held it against her ear and clicked the button on the base where the phone had rested. There was no dial tone. She stabbed at the button several more times, with no results.

"Dammit."

She tried to set the phone back on its cradle. It slipped from her hand and clattered to the floor.

"Shit."

She picked it up and noticed a red smear on its side. The red stain stood out against the white plastic of the phone. Looking at the hardwood floor, she noticed red splotches. They trailed away to the door at the back of the room. She wiped the side of the phone against her leg and replaced it on its hook.

"Excuse me? Who are you?"

Candy pivoted away from the fireplace, her hand over her heart. "Oh, my. I'm so sorry, I am, um, my name is Candy. I called out several times. I knocked on the door and when no one answered I opened your door. I'm sorry, I was freezing and…" Candy faced a heavy-set woman whose face held an empty expression. Upon noticing the woman's jowls, Candy thought of Max, the bulldog who lived across the hall in her apartment building. Max's cheeks also hung low, and he usually looked as distant and thoughtless as the woman before her.

The woman was watching her, but did not seem concerned that Candy stood in her living room. She was heavyset, appeared to be in her thirties, had short brown hair, pale green eyes, and wore a sizeable amount of lipstick. She had an apron wrapped around a simple blue dress and stood barefoot.

Candy noticed several red spots and smears that stained her white apron. They appeared to be from the same source as the spots on the floor. The woman's hands were also crusted with red.

"Anyway, I was freezing because my car got stuck out on the highway. It's a route I travel often, and I had remembered your home and decided to try to walk here. I was afraid I would get lost. I was so frozen that I was getting worried. When I saw your phone over here, I thought I could call my son, but the phone doesn't seem to work."

The woman nodded, "Uh-huh. It's the storm. It's been out all morning." She continued to gaze at Candy as though she were trying to remember if they had met before.

Candy smiled. "I couldn't help myself with your fire burning. I'm sorry for intruding. I'm soaking wet. I've never done this before, I promise. I was desperate."

The woman nodded again and smiled. "Where's my manners? I'm Margaret. Folks mostly call me Margie though." She extended a dirty hand to Candy. "No worries in breaking into my house, and Larry, that's my husband, he won't mind either." Margie motioned to the door at the back of the room.

Candy shook her hand and said, "Well, thank you for your understanding. I thought I might die out there. By the way, whatever you're making sure smells good."

Coming Up Short 9

Candy wiped her hand on the back of her jeans, when she was sure Margie wouldn't notice. She could feel stickiness on her palm. The grime seemed to come off with the moisture in her pants.

Margie smiled and then giggled. The placid, uninterested expression had evaporated. She stopped and forced her grin away but couldn't contain it, and laughed again. She waved a hand at Candy, "Oh, Lordy, ain't you a sight?"

Candy chuckled. "Yes, I'm afraid I must be. Like I said, it's bad out there." She felt uncomfortable around the woman. Something wasn't quite right about her. The energy she put off was frenetic, as though she had been caught in something she preferred to keep secret. Moments before, she had been vacant.

Margie rubbed a hand across her chin and lips, smearing red goop across her face.

Candy pointed and said, "You have a little, uh… there on your face."

"Huh?" Margie held her hand out before her and then rubbed it on her apron, creating a larger stain.

"Oh, oopsie, I was making a.... tell you what. Hold on a moment. You must be half-starved."

The woman disappeared through the door, stepping on the red stains on the floor.

Candy forced her winter cap back onto her head and began shoving her hands back into her wet gloves. She had to find a way to communicate with Matt, and the storm was only getting worse. She couldn't afford to linger in the home much longer.

As she finished, the woman entered the room holding a bread roll with steaming grilled meat and peppers stuffed inside. "Here you go." She appraised Candy's hat and gloves. "Why not stay a little longer and warm up before you leave?"

Candy accepted the sandwich. It smelled delicious. "I would, but my son will be worried about me. I need to find a phone somewhere. I better get moving again." Candy pointed to the food resting in her gloved hand. "Thank you for this, it smells delicious."

Margie laughed and winked at her. "My name is Margie, by the way."

Coming Up Short 9

Candy only smiled, not wanting to tell the woman she had already shared her name.

"That's from a Larry steak I made." Margie rolled her eyes and said, "I got myself all turned up…" She giggled again. "I meant it's from a Larry steak I made for Larry."

The woman tilted her head toward the ceiling and repeated what she had said while counting on her fingers. "Oh geez, no, oopsie, I meant it's a Larry Steak for Larry, my husband, for dinner." She paused and then asked Candy, "I said that wrong again." She smacked herself on her forehead. "I meant, it's from, a steak… I. Made. For. Larry." She sighed, "There you go, got it right that time."

Margie giggled again and held a hand over her mouth. "Sometimes I get a little silly. Larry says it's unbecoming." She balled up her fists and bent her arms at her sides, mimicking her husband. She lowered her voice and said, "Margie, acting like that will have folks thinking them cows in the barn have more dang sense in their heads than you." Margie snorted and said, "Isn't that a great impersonation of him?"

Coming Up Short 9

Candy nodded and stepped past the woman. "Yes, it sure is. I can see him in my mind."

Margie stopped laughing as Candy opened the front door and said, "But you've never met him."

Stepping onto the freezing front porch, Candy replied, "Of course, but I can sure imagine him. Listen, thank you again for your hospitality and the sandwich. I was starving. By the way, any idea of where I could walk to a phone?"

Wind swooped across the front porch, pieces of stray hair sweeping her face.

Margie pointed up the road in the direction Candy had been walking. "That way. The Laziest Dog Saloon. It's the nearest place. It's not far." Her eyes glazed over. "Me and Larry used to go get drinks up there once in a while, but that's when I was thin."

Margie shut the door in her face. Candy could hear the woman laughing inside and calling out to her husband, "Larry! It's dinnertime!"

Candy smelled the sandwich. Her stomach

rumbled in response. Margie was a weird woman and Candy was suspicious of her strange behavior, but she had to eat. She would never have enough energy to wade through the storm without sustenance.

She bit into the sandwich as she walked across the porch.

"Oh, God, that's good. You're a strange one, Margie, but you can frickin cook."

She took another bite, juice from the tender meat dribbling down her chin. The cold was moving through her coat again, but she didn't notice. She consumed the pepper-flavored meat and tender bread.

Before she had stomped her way back to the two-lane highway, the sandwich was gone. She thought of the name of the business that Margie had given her. The Laziest Dog Saloon.

She shuddered. "Why does it have to be a bar?"

THREE

Coming Up Short 9

Margie pushed open the door that led from the living room into the kitchen. She stared at Larry, who she had shackled to the top of the kitchen table. It had been a nasty chore getting his unconscious body lifted there. Good thing she had gained some weight over the past few years. Larry called it the lead in her ass.

"You won't be saying rude things to me anymore, will you?" She asked him, knowing he could not respond.

He tracked her movements across the kitchen with his eyes. He couldn't move his head. It was strapped down, as well as his arms and legs. She had also gagged him, although he stilled, tried to plead with her through his mumbling. Of course, he only mumbled when he was conscious. Each time she had gotten some steak from him, he had passed out.

"Not as tough as you let on after all, are you, Lawrence?" She giggled. "You know what's so funny? If you think about it, all the steaks I fried up for you through the years, helped make your own steaks. It's like the process of life or something." She poked him in the fleshless, exposed section of his abdomen and he squealed, straining at his binds. "You don't get it, Larry. It's like, Larry eats a steak, and he grows one in his own body. I did not know that cooking for you all those years, I was actually preparing food for the apocalypse. You didn't know that either, did you?"

Margie grabbed a wet cloth and wiped some of Larry's blood from the table.

"Jesus warned us that the end times were coming, and he did that thousands of years ago." She laughed and said, "Of course, you don't know nothing about that Mr. Larry, because you refused to come to church with me and hear the words of the lord."

She picked up her butcher knife. Larry's eyes grew wide. He wriggled against the ropes that held him in place.

"Shh, settle yourself down there, Lawrence." She laughed again, louder this time. "What I can't figure out is why this is all so funny." She snickered against the backside of her hand and leaned against the table. "Larry steaks. That's just about the funniest dang thing." She sat next to him. "Larry steaks. Barry, Larry, and you are bare, aren't you?"

She laid her forehead against the open wound in his gut. His eyes rolled for a moment in his head and then settled back into place. He cried against the wadded-up underwear she had stuffed into his mouth.

"Barry, Larry, the steak-bearing man." She laughed harder, wiping at a tear that had wandered free of her eye. "Oh, Lord, it's so... dang... funny." She doubled over again in a laughing fit. Her hair brushed his wound. He tried to scream.

She sat up. "Barry, Larry, the steak-bearing man, bearing them steaks as fast as he can." Her shoulders bounced up and down with her chuckles.

"Now, let's get us some more of that good meat." She paused, holding the knife over his body. "Good day, good meat, good Lord, let's eat!"

Larry thrashed against the top of the table.

"Now, you hush. I had to share that last meat with a nice lady who was finding her way in the storm. So now, mama is hungry." She stood up and swatted herself on the ass. "And as you said yourself, it takes a great deal of food to keep up this girth."

Margie backed away from the table. Larry's eyes tracked her. A fine layer of sweat had broken out across his forehead. As she moved, she made beeping sounds.

"It's like the warning on those trucks that carry the extra-wide loads. Isn't that what you said, Larry? I have a wide load back here?" She beeped her way to the table, laughed, and then leaned close to his face. "Beep, beep, BEEP!"

Margie laid the cold steel of her bloodied blade against the hole in Larry's stomach. Larry made a humming sound under his gag.

Margie chuckled and pushed the knife into his flesh. "Now, you be still. It's time for Margie to have herself a good Larry steak, medium-rare." She pushed the knife around until it stuck against a rib.

Larry cried out, twisting against her cutting, until he finally lost consciousness.

Laughers

Available on Amazon! Now available on Amazon!

Coming Up Short 9

Thank you

Thank you for reading *Coming Up Short 9*. *Coming Up Short 9* takes place in many locations, mostly in Colorado. While some of the locations in *Coming Up Short 9* are real places, others are entirely fictitious. The specific locations and addresses are not real, and all characters are also fictitious.

The ideas for *Coming Up Short 9* came from a variety of places. I had published *Coming Up Short*, the first volume not knowing if there would be much of an audience for a collection of dark tales. I have always been a fan of horror anthologies, and the truth is, sometimes a great idea will pop into my head, but it isn't enough story to become a novel. I had several short stories in various stages of development and thought they were too good to sit on the sidelines. I pressed the publish button with the thought that I might regret it, but time would tell.

Over the past couple of years, multiple books in this series have spent time at number one on the Amazon charts. I've been stunned by the reception to these short works and I'm grateful to each and every one of you for taking the time to not only read but rate and review these books.

You have my undying gratitude.

Coming Up Short 9

So, a little background on some of the stories in *Coming Up Short 9*.

Queller – I had a scene in my head, and I couldn't get rid of it. In it, I saw a woman try on an antique ring and struggle to get it off. Once she was able to finally remove it, there was a word pressed into her skin from inside the ring. I wasn't sure what the word was, exactly, but I wondered what would happen if this word, while imprinted on her, altered her behavior in some way. Of course, it would take her a while to realize this because the power of that word would fade with the diminishment of the imprinting. That led me to the idea that it would happen again, and that the devil would be the cause of it. If you've read any of the previous installments in this series, you know I love to write the Lived character.

False Deprivation – I have always wondered about the use of sensory deprivation in the treatment of various psychological ailments. The topic provides ample opportunity for nefarious and dark complications. In this instance, my goal was to create a little confusion on our way to the reveal at the end. That our main character was in the tank the entire time was the idea that finally prompted me to write this story.

KoK – I get a lot of email from people demanding the next book in the Killer of Killer series after every release in that series. People love

Kalen and Mitchell and their very antagonistic, but secretly loving relationship, and so do I. I wanted to do something on the shorter, and slightly lighter side, and this is the story that came out of that desire. It began with a dream in which Kalen was holding a man hostage in his car, and when I woke up, I realized, though this would seem to be a bad thing to do, Kalen would of course have a purpose and that purpose would be to protect the innocent. I hope this story quenches your KoK appetite until book 11 is unleashed on the world.

Thank you again for reading! I hope you enjoy these stories as much as I enjoy writing them!

As we part for now, I have a request for you my fellow reader of horror and thrillers. **PLEASE** take a moment to write a review on Amazon.

PRETTY PLEASE!!!

AND if I can't twist your arm behind your back with all my begging for a review…maybe you'd consider a quick rating. Rating anything on Amazon is a 10 second mission of simply clicking on a star (Ahem, I like the 5th star the best, in case you were wondering.)

Please and in advance, much thanks!

I would also love to invite you to join our **Preferred Reader Club and Newsletter** at www.withinthefogbook.com

Coming Up Short 9

Preferred readers get first looks at my latest works, and I enjoy sending club members signed copies of books sometimes as a way of saying thank you.

As always, beware of the things that lurk in the dark. Keep your eyes and ears open. Strange events and happenings are all around us…

Evil things happen and they're caused by evil people and monsters.

One step too close to the edge of the shadows will have them reaching for you.

They're waiting, fangs exposed, drooling as they anticipate the delicious taste of your supple flesh…

And most likely, Lived Southerly has something to do with their presence.

See you soon.

Charles Welch

12/3/24

Coming Up Short 9

ABOUT THE AUTHOR

Charles Welch lives in Greeley, CO. He is a former public-school teacher and holds an M.Ed. in Learning and Technology and an Ed.D. in eLearning. He lives with his wife Mia and has 3 children, 5 god children and 3 grandchildren. His passions include the Denver Broncos, reading the masters of horror and watching every scary movie he can.

Printed in Great Britain
by Amazon